Against her will, her lips were parting...

Suddenly it was as though some unbelievably wonderful fireworks had exploded in her mind, showering brilliance and color throughout the darkness. She found her back arching upward, thrusting her breasts against his hard chest.

Her fingers clenched in his hair—and then she was lost in a kiss more utterly sensual, more bone-melting than anything she had ever dreamed of. His body was fierce and hard against hers, their mouths locked together in a sweetness that was scalding, enveloping her like fire....

"Jason," she gasped as he drew back to smile down at her. "Don't do this to me! Let me up!"

"Stop playing the innocent," he purred. "Your kisses tell me everything I want to know, Storm Calderwood."

HARLEQUIN PRESENTS
by Madeleine Ker

These books may be available at your local bookseller.

For a free catalog listing all titles currently available,
send your name and address to:

Harlequin Reader Service
P.O. Box 52040, Phoenix, AZ   85072-9988
Canadian address: Stratford, Ontario   N5A 6W2

MADELEINE KER

---

virtuous lady

Harlequin Books

TORONTO · NEW YORK · LONDON
AMSTERDAM · PARIS · SYDNEY · HAMBURG
STOCKHOLM · ATHENS · TOKYO · MILAN

Harlequin Presents first edition January 1984
ISBN 0-373-10656-4

Original hardcover edition published in 1983
by Mills & Boon Limited

CHAPTER ONE

'You actually *struck* the Prince?' said Miss Quinlan faintly. 'The Sheik's only son—you *actually* struck him?'

Storm nodded glumly.

'Yes, Miss Quinlan. It was just a smack on the bottom, though. I don't know why they made such a fuss about it.' She shifted uncomfortably in her chair; Miss Quinlan's employment agency didn't stretch to anything so un-genteel as comfortable chairs. Especially not for recently-sacked employees. She met Miss Quinlan's baleful eyes defiantly. 'Besides,' she added, 'he thoroughly deserved it.'

'He was a Prince of the blood Royal!' squawked Miss Quinlan in outrage.

'He was a little monster,' said Storm.

Miss Quinlan bridled.

'Your duty as the child's governess,' she said frigidly 'was to educate him—not to administer corporal punishment! I really cannot imagine what *possessed* you . . .'

Storm waited patiently for Miss Quinlan to finish. Of the whole three months she had spent in Saudi Arabia, the only bright spot had been the moment when she had tipped the astonished Prince—aged ten—over her knee, and had delivered the controversial smack. At first sight, three months before, the job of governess to a rich oil-sheik's only son had seemed an absolute plum. Miss Quinlan had painted Storm's future career in glowing terms—excitement, glamour, golden sun, easy hours, splendid salary, the chance of working in an Eastern palace—it had all sounded so wonderful.

What Miss Quinlan *hadn't* mentioned was that Storm was the fifth governess she had sent to the same family in two years.

And it hadn't taken Storm more than a day to work out that the Saudi job was no plum.

Oh, the palace was luxury itself, and no one could possibly complain about the salary. And if you obeyed the strict Saudi code of ethics, it was a pleasant enough country. But the young Prince Majeed Hassan Hussein, heir to the Sheik's oil millions and Storm's only charge, was the closest thing to a fiend in human shape that Storm had ever set eyes on.

'Are you listening to me, Miss Calderwood?' Miss Quinlan rapped out.

'Yes, Miss Quinlan,' Storm said quietly. She was not inclined to feel particularly kindly towards Miss Quinlan. She should have warned Storm, said something at least.

Spoiled from birth, pampered in his every whim, the little Prince reacted to any opposition with spectacular tantrums and fits. In those moods, the Palace servants simply fled. But not Storm Calderwood. Poor fool that she was, she had taken her job seriously, had tried to control the little brute, had tried to make him eat his vegetables, do his sums, and go to bed at bedtime.

Had put up with the kicks to the ankles, the scratches and bites, the sharp little punches that Majeed Hassan Hussein was so expert at delivering.

But two months of such saintly restraint had worn her patience thin—as it had worn the patience of the four other governesses who had preceded her. When the Prince had butted her in the stomach one day, winding her completely, Storm had had enough. As soon as she had recovered her breath, she had advanced on Majeed Hassan Hussein with the light of battle in her eye. She had only delivered one smack. Her heart had failed her after that—Storm was incapable of wanting to really hurt any living creature. She was certain that the Prince had hardly felt it, anyway; but the blow to his princely pride had been severe, and had precipitated a tantrum of such dimensions that Storm had found herself escorted out of the Palace with almost indecent haste within hours.

The odd thing was that the little Prince had been genuinely sorry to see her go, presenting her with a box of sticky dates to eat on the flight home.

'*Salaam aleikum*, Miss Calderwood,' he had said shyly. Well, Allah help the next poor unsuspecting governess who went there.

'You've let me down *very* badly,' Miss Quinlan was concluding self-righteously.

'But, Miss Quinlan,' Storm said tentatively, 'I think you might have told me that I was the fifth governess to be sent there. It would have given me some warning about what to expect—'

'How dare you?' Miss Quinlan snorted. 'You came to me without references of any kind, Miss Calderwood! I took you on face value, trusting you to hold the name of Quinlan's high—'

'I know,' Storm interrupted, 'but I wasn't expecting the Prince to be quite so unmanageable. I really think you could have given me some idea . . .' She tailed off, fighting back her desire to put it all a lot more strongly. It wouldn't do, after all, to offend old Miss Quinlan. Storm was rather hoping that she would be able to find her another job. The Calderwood exchequer was going to be in need of funds from now on.

'Well, that can't be helped now,' Miss Quinlan retorted. 'You've been a *great* disappointment to me. When I took you on, practically off the streets'—Storm gritted her teeth, but said nothing—'I had the *highest* hopes for your career. What possessed you to behave so stupidly I *cannot* think. You've let Quinlan's down badly, Miss Calderwood—very badly indeed!'

'But—'

'And it's no use trying say that Quinlan's let *you* down,' Miss Quinlan added in a quivering contralto. 'I consider that *very* ungrateful.'

'I'm sorry, Miss Quinlan,' Storm sighed.

'It is fortunate that you got off with a mere dismissal.' She fixed Storm with her yellow eye. 'Did you consider,' she said with grim relish, 'that the Sheik might have ordered your hands to be cut off?'

'No,' admitted Storm, glancing at her decidedly pretty hands, 'that aspect of it hadn't occurred to me.'

'No. Nor, I presume, did you pause to consider the reputation of Quinlan's Employment Agency before you started beating this child?'

'I didn't exactly beat him,' Storm corrected, beginning to feel annoyed. 'I gave him one light smack. After all, he has left quite a bruise on my stomach, you know!'

'I am not *interested* in your stomach,' Miss Quinlan said frostily. She scooped up the file on her desk with an angry claw, and dropped it into the waste-paper basket. The cover read 'S. L. Calderwood'. Storm blinked in dismay.

'That is *that*, Miss Calderwood. I must inform you that
Quinlan's does not employ staff who are in the habit of
striking children. You have damaged the reputation of
this agency once, Miss Calderwood. Let us hope that we
can salvage *something* from the wreckage.' Miss Quinlan
made it sound as though Storm had piloted a Concorde
through the roof of the dingy (but genteel) little office.
'You shall certainly not be permitted to damage our
reputation again.'

'You—you mean—I'm fired?'

'I should have thought that was *perfectly* obvious,'
said Miss Quinlan, rising.

Storm stood up slowly, blinking.

'Miss Quinlan—'

'That will be *quite* enough,' said Miss Quinlan coldly.
'If the Sheik decides to take legal action, I shall know
where to find you. *Good*bye.'

'But, Miss Quinlan—'

'There is no more to be said, Miss Calderwood,' she
replied, and pushed Storm firmly to the door.

Dazed, Storm walked out into the colour and noise of
Bond Street, and tried to consider her position. The
golden tan from the Middle East was still on her skin,
and her sweet, oval face and green eyes attracted plenty
of male glances as she wandered along the pavement.
There was, she calculated, about fifty pounds in her
bank account. Within a few days—unless the Sheik
stopped payment—there should be about two hundred
more coming through the Bank of Arabia. She was
comfortably off. For the time being. And she had the
flat. For the time being. Storm wandered into a little
coffee-bar and sat down to brood over her Cappuccino.
Well, she was on the road again. Two months as a

governess, and the end of another dream. The last thing had been waitressing in a coffee-bar very like this one. How dreadfully dull that been. That had lasted six months, though—not bad for a child-beater. And before the waitress job it had been—what had it been? Had it been the tempting job for the secretarial agency? Or the fruit-shop where the man had pinched her bottom?

The thing was that when you were very pretty, inclined to be impetuous—and when a doting father had christened you Storm—you entered any career with a disadvantage.

Emerging from a red-brick university at the absurdly young age of twenty, with no parents to guide her, no fortune to sustain her, and no prospective husband to tame her, Storm Calderwood had embarked on a miniodyssey of jobs. Startlingly pretty, with hair that really was golden, and eyes that really were emerald, she had nevertheless been too short for modelling. And not vain enough for acting, advertising or publicity-agenting. And not—well, just not anything. The very first job she had taken, with the electrical firm, had been ominously suggestive of things to come. Her immediate boss had sneered at her literature-and-Italian degree, and had set her to work filing and typing. Soul-deadening work, that had been a bad let-down after three years at university, expecting a waiting world to simply throw itself at her feet once she had graduated. The simple fact was that there just weren't any jobs. Not jobs for young women who didn't know anything more than a few dozen good books to read and a working knowledge of Italian literature in the twentieth century. Not even jobs for startlingly pretty young women with green eyes. There were just boring jobs, mind-destroying jobs, jobs that no one else wanted, or that were only going for six weeks until our Mrs Simpson gets back, or where the boss was a sex-maniac, or where—

Storm was beginning to regret that very satisfying smack to Prince Majeed's wicked little bottom. In retrospect—and when you found yourself unemployed all of a sudden in a drizzly London autumn—even Prince Majeed was a better prospect than nothing. And those magnificent dinners! She leaned back, and winced suddenly at the twinge in her solar plexus, where the Royal head had struck with such demonic accuracy. No, on second thoughts, nothing *was* a better prospect than Prince Majeed. But she was going to have to get moving again—and soon. Money simply evaporated when there wasn't a steady supply coming in.

She paid for her Cappuccino, and went straight to the nearest cashpoint outside her bank, inserted her card, and punched out a request for her balance. BALANCE ON 20TH OCTOBER £29.05 CR, said the machine impassively. Oh. Less than she had expected. Rather more downcast, Storm took a bus back to Maida Vale, did some shopping at the local supermarket, stared back at the gum-chewing young man behind the till, and went up to her flat.

'Pokey' wasn't a nice word. Which was why the landlord had described it as 'compact'. Still, she thought, loading eggs and bacon into the fridge (which rattled and snarled at night like an electric ghost) it was home. Literally, home. When her parents had died, leaving Storm a bewildered sixteen-year-old, their house had gone, too. This flat was the last of many such digs she had lived in. And it was a far cry from the luxury of the Sheik's mansion!

She checked her watch. There was time to telephone Kelly Oates, her best friend, and tell her that she was back in London. She dialled the number of the florist's shop where Kelly worked, and it was Kelly's slightly breathless voice which answered at the fourth ring.

'Kelly? It's good to hear your voice again!'

'Storm! Where are you calling from?'

'My flat in Maida Vale.'

'*Maida Vale?* I thought you were still in Arabia! What happened to your job? Oh no—you haven't got the sack again, have you?'

'I'm afraid so,' Storm said glumly.

'What did you do, you chump? Steal the Crown Jewels?'

'I smacked the Prince,' she confessed.

'Oh. Is that serious?'

'Apparently so,' Storm smiled. 'They hustled me out of the country in twenty-four hours flat. But tell me about yourself—what's the news?'

'Oh, there's great news,' Kelly laughed mysteriously, 'but that can wait until I see you. Have you told Miss Quinlan about your disaster?'

'Yes,' groaned Storm.

'What did she say?'

'Guess,' rejoined Storm ruefully. 'And she's refused to try and find me another job—says I've ruined their reputation.'

'Oh, nonsense,' said Kelly firmly. 'But how's your financial situation? Are the bailiffs at the door?'

'Not as bad as that,' sighed Storm. 'I'll tell you when I see you. Fancy bacon and eggs for lunch—at my flat?'

'I'll be there in half an hour.'

'I'm dying to see you, Kelly!'

'Me, too. I'll pick up a couple of mousses at the supermarket. So long!'

Storm whiled away the time waiting for Kelly by looking through the jobs in that morning's paper. It was the old story—a hundred and twenty words per minute would have been of infinitely more value than an arts B.A. And Storm's meagre seventy w.p.m. was too erratic for even the most undemanding office work. Tentatively, she circled two ads, hesitated, then rang the first. The job had already been taken.

'Already?' gasped Storm.

'Times are hard,' said the middle-aged voice sympathetically, and rang off. Storm looked at the second ad she had circled. Another shop assistant's job. Except that this one promised 'interesting and rewarding work for the right person.' She dialled the number wearily. It was a Soho sex-shop.

'I don't think I'm the right person,' she assured the husky-voiced man, and hung up. She was lost in glum thoughts when Kelly knocked on the door. The friends embraced affectionately. Kelly and Storm had corresponded faithfully throughout Storm's Middle Eastern job though Storm had, she recalled guiltily, rather over-glamourised her situation in her letters home.

'You've still got the flat, I see,' said Kelly breathlessly, sitting her neat person gingerly on an extremely dusty sofa.

'I signed a year's lease,' Storm explained, 'so I kept up the payments while I was in the Middle East. I suppose I could have let it out—but somehow I didn't fancy the idea of someone else living here.'

'Anyway, never mind all that! Storm, you look absolutely fabulous, my dear. You could go straight on a poster advertising holidays in sunny Spain! So tell me—what went wrong this time?'

Storm explained as concisely as she could as she grilled bacon and fried eggs. As they sat down to the meal together, Kelly shook her brown head ruefully.

'Honestly, Storm, I'm beginning to think you're unemployable. What on earth possessed you to hit the little brute?'

'I didn't hit him—I'm not a monster, for heaven's sake—I only smacked him. And I'll bet it hurt my hand a lot more than it hurt young Majeed's—'

'And supposing Sheik Whatsit had taken into his head to give you a public flogging? Or have you stoned to death for touching the Royal person?'

'That's what old Miss Quinlan said. Pass the Worcester sauce, please. Oh, I don't know,' Storm continued, thumping the bottle with her palm, 'I suppose he could have done something like that. I just lost my temper.'

'You're always losing your temper, Storm.'

'That's not true! I—oh, hell!' A grisly plug of congealed sauce plopped out of the neck of the bottle, and a brown flood covered her eggs. Kelly looked at the result with ill-concealed disgust.

'Has that sauce been sitting here since you left for the Middle East two months ago?' she asked.

'I guess so. How did you know?' asked Storm, scraping some of the flood off the tablecloth.

'There's all green mould on the label, that's how I know,' retorted Kelly. She pushed her plate away, and regarded her friend with patient resignation. 'Storm, forget lunch. Let's just have some coffee, and talk. Okay?'

'Okay,' sighed Storm. She looked at Kelly with affec-

tionate green eyes. 'I'm always in the soup, Kelly, aren't
I? And I'm sorry about the lunch.'

'Never mind,' smiled Kelly, carefully dusting the sofa
this time before she sat in it. Kelly was looking very well,
Storm realised. Her mousy hair was glossy and thick,
and her normally pale skin was glowing, as though with
inner life. Some man was probably in the background,
she thought as she made the coffee. It was not until she
passed Kelly her cup that she noticed the sparkle on her
friend's finger.

'Kelly! You're engaged!'

'I wondered when you'd notice,' laughed Kelly,
accepting the kiss. 'Only since last week.'

'Who is he?'

'Paul Phillips. He works at Guy's.'

'A doctor?'

Kelly nodded, her hazel eyes bright.

'The best-looking doctor in London. *And* the kind-
est.'

'Are you happy?' asked Storm unnecessarily, casting
a wistful glance at her friend's glowing face.

'I'm over the moon! We're getting married after
Christmas.'

'Fantastic! I suppose this has been a whirlwind
romance?'

Kelly nodded. 'I've only known him for six weeks. But
I'm so sure he's the one, Storm—I've never met anyone
like him in my life—he's—he's—' She drew a deep
breath with shining eyes. 'Oh, he's just wonderful, that's
all.'

'How I envy you,' said Storm quietly, smiling rather
sadly at Kelly.

'No, you don't,' said Kelly briskly. 'You always said

marriage wasn't for you, and it isn't. Not yet, anyway. What you need, my girl, is to settle down and sort your confused self out.'

Storm took her hand to examine the sparkling stone.

'What I need is a *job*. That's a beautiful ring, Kelly.' She restored her friend's hand admiringly. 'I can't wait to meet your Paul. Is he handsome? Clever?'

'He's a cross between Einstein and Cary Grant,' grinned Kelly. 'You'll like him.'

'I'll bet I will. It's been absolute ages since I've met a really attractive man—you lucky thing!'

'Oh, Paul's wonderful,' Kelly breathed, and Storm hid her smile. Love would make Paul seem wonderful to Kelly even if he were the ugliest man on earth. 'What about you?' Kelly probed. 'Did you meet any gorgeous Rudolph Valentino types out in the desert?'

'Huh! The only male I ever saw was the Prince—and he was more like a miniature Boris Karloff.'

'That's what you need,' Kelly judged smugly. 'Love. Some wonderful, masterful man to set you to rights—'

'Love is a mental aberration,' Storm grinned. 'It's bad for the brain, Kelly. Anyway, I'm far too sensible to want to be dominated by some brute of a male chauvinist pig. Anyway,' she sighed, 'what I need is a job, not a man. Though I must say, the thought of going back to work horrifies me. I haven't had a holiday for years. I seem to have been working for ever.'

Kelly nodded sympathetically.

'You say you've got enough to tide you over? Paul and I could always lend you—'

'Thanks, Kelly,' smiled Storm, 'but I'm all right for the time being. If I end up starving, I'll take you up on that offer.'

'I wonder,' mused Kelly, 'whether you're really suited for the job market. You're not exactly run-of-the-mill, you know. Perhaps—well, perhaps instead of going out looking for a job, why not let the jobs come looking for you?'

Storm's green eyes met hers in puzzlement.

'How?'

'By putting an ad in the paper. After all, you've never found a job yet that suited you. So why not advertise? Something like, "Girl, 22, seeks interesting and rewarding employment." How about it?'

'It's an idea,' said Storm with a grin, showing very white, very even teeth. 'But what about all the crazies and weirdos who're bound to answer?'

'Well, you don't put your name in or anything—just a box number. Then you sort through them, in privacy, and at your leisure. You never know what'll turn up.'

Storm's eyes had begun to sparkle with interest. She jumped up to get a writing-pad and a pencil.

'I think you've hit on something, Kelly. Help me draw up the wording.'

'Well, I'd try "Girl, 22—"'—no, better make that "Young person, 22—"'

'I like *Girl, 22*,' grinned Storm.

'How about *lady*?' Kelly compromised.

'Right,' said Storm, writing busily, '*Lady, 22, seeks employment. Must be unusual and interesting. Nothing illegal.* How's that?'

'Not bad,' said Kelly, smiling at Storm affectionately. 'I'd put it in the evening papers, rather than the morning ones.'

'I can't afford to put it in more than one or two papers,' said Storm, surveying her composition critically. 'How about one evening, one morning paper?'

'*Standard* and *Times*?'

'*The Standard* and *The Times* it is,' said Storm. She looked up at Kelly with a happy face. 'Do you know, Kelly, I think you've hit on a terrific idea here!'

'I endeavour to give satisfaction,' said Kelly with a smile, and glanced at her watch. 'Oh dear, I must fly. What are you doing tonight?'

'Moping. Why?'

'Come out with me and Paul—I'm dying for you to meet him.'

'I'm dying to meet him myself,' said Storm, following her friend to the door. 'Shall I come round to your place?'

'No, we'll pick you up. About eight? Great! Now get on the line to those newspapers!'

Storm stared after Kelly's hurrying figure, smiling to herself; then closed the door, and went back to her advertisement and a second cup of coffee. The more she thought about it, the more intriguing the idea was beginning to sound. She chewed her pencil for half an hour, and eventually settled on:

Virtuous lady, 22, seeks unusual or interesting employment. Prepared to consider anything not illegal or boring. Immediate reply guaranteed.

She took her pad to the telephone, and made two calls, one to *The Times*, the other to the *Standard*. The secretary at *The Times* was noncommittal. The woman at the *Standard* said dubiously, 'You'll get a lot of creeps answering *that* ad, dearie.' For a few pounds, both papers agreed to let her use a box number, and she arranged to pick her mail up at the newspaper offices. Then she sat down.

A strange, familiar feeling came over her. What was it? Something from her childhood . . . Yes, that was it. It was the feeling they used to get when they—Storm and her friends and Katey her cousin—had sat down around the ouija board. How clearly she remembered it—the darkened room, the little round table with all the letters of the alphabet round its edges (belonging to Katey's mother, and forbidden to little girls). And the five or six faces sitting in delicious terror around it, each with a trembling finger on the glass, waiting for it to scrape its way eerily from letter to letter in the exciting, ghostly dark.

The others had usually been too nervous to start, and it was Storm who asked the first questions, grubby forefinger waiting on the glass—*is there anybody there?* And then there was the expectant pause, the nervous giggles, before the glass scraped and slithered its way round the letters.

It was that sense of waiting that she recalled now, the anticipation, the nervousness. She walked to the window, and stared out at rainy, shiny streets. And wondered who, in the great unknown world out there, was going to answer her advertisement.

CHAPTER TWO

READING her own advertisement in the next morning's *Times* gave her a strange feeling. Her entry looked so odd in the sober columns, and as she read through the Situations Wanted entries, she realised that there were none as peculiar as hers. There was the gamekeeper, the two nannies, the experienced salesperson, and the qualified accountant, all with their respectable, drab entries. Among them, hers was as bizarre and frivolous as a butterfly in a second-hand bookshop. Still, reading it gave her a tingle of excitement.

The previous evening with Kelly and Paul had been fun. Paul had turned out to be a thin, vaguely good-looking young man with a bright line in funny remarks. Storm had thoroughly approved of him—he was just perfect for Kelly. And by the moony looks they kept exchanging, they were utterly in love with one another. Which was a condition Storm was inclined to find slightly incomprehensible. She had once fancied herself besotted by one of her tutors in her first year at university—but that had soon passed, revealing him to be a rather moth-eaten old bachelor, very far from the Byronesque figure of her fantasies. Since then, she had been out with plenty of young men, and had had to fight off not less than half of them in parked cars or in the cinema—but had never really felt her heart beat any quicker over any of them. She obviously just wasn't cut out for romance and flirtation. Moonlight and roses left her cold. And anyway, she had always had plenty of other things to worry about, like where her next square meal was coming from.

So she had watched Kelly and Paul with a patient smile, not really understanding. Paul had been amused and impressed with their idea regarding Storm's ad. And he had looked at her with assessing blue eyes (did all doctors have those clinical eyes? she wondered) and had said, 'You're even more beautiful than Kelly led me to believe,' which was nice of him.

It had been her mother, of course, who had given Storm her beautiful oval face and blonde hair. From her father had come the sparkling green eyes and the independent disposition. Poor Mum and Dad! She had scarcely begun to get close to them, after the cold war of adolescence, when they had taken that ill-fated drive up to Scotland. Where the long, treacherous slick of oil lurking on a rainy road had plunged them into the barrier, and down the little ravine into the glen below. A flustered, kindly nurse had told Storm a sentimental story about how they had bade her goodbye in hospital before taking the voyage into the unknown; but a brusque doctor had dispelled that friendly lie by informing her that neither of them had regained consciousness before they died. As pointless and as tragic as that.

She shook the sad thoughts out of her blonde head. It had been years since she had allowed herself to remember the incidents of that horrible month. She surveyed the flat with the light of battle in her eyes. Two long months of neglect had made it practically unliveable, and she had sneezed all night with the dust. She tied a pinafore around her waist, plugged in the Hoover, and spent the day cleaning.

By the time she had done, the flat was spotless again, every surface gleaming, each cushion plumped, every pane of glass as clean as daylight. She spent the evening watching television, her long, pretty legs stretched out on the pouffe, eating apples. With great self-control, she resisted the urge to pick up her mail the next day, knowing there would be more to look through if she waited an extra twenty-four hours. But the day after that, she took the Tube in to Fleet Street, her heart beating with excitement. She was staggered at the amount of mail that was waiting for her—a great pile of assorted envelopes and cards at each office. Excited, she bore her treasure home in triumph, made a large pot of tea, and sat down with gleaming eyes to sort through the collection.

The vast majority proved to be instantly disappointing—letters from various fanatical religious organisations, several from door-to-door selling firms promising huge profits, three or four from perverts, one or two from organisations willing to lend her money at rates that would have made Shylock blench. These she discarded, leaving a handful of letters which contained genuine job offers—or which were otherwise interesting. There was even a proposal of marriage among these. And various unspecified jobs in unspecified foreign countries. An offer from a man who needed a female partner in a balloon race. A man who wanted someone to crew for him in a trans-Atlantic yacht voyage. A woman who wanted a partner to go prospecting for opals in Mexico. Somebody called K. K. Kavanagh (sex unknown) who wanted to launch a satirical magazine in Scotland. And a letter from Kelly Oates, saying 'Dear Storm, this is just to comfort you in case nobody else replies to your ad . . .'

She brooded over her collection, slowly discarding the ones that seemed the least promising, or the most suspicious.

Among the first to go was the proposal of marriage, a curtly-written note that was the most unromantic thing Storm had ever read. The trans-Atlantic yacht voyage sounded too cold an exploit for the autumn. The balloon race sounded delightfully impractical and unusual—but would it bring in any much-needed funds? She laid it to one side thoughtfully. Opal-hunting in Mexico sounded delightfully romantic. But a little rough. Which left the satirical magazine (was there really a market for satire in Scotland?) and various unspecified jobs in foreign parts. Including the gentleman who signed himself Mustapha Freedom, and who wanted nurses to tend the wounded 'in the freedom struggle for our newly-developed but oppressed nation'. After second thoughts, she discarded this one as well, and went to phone Kelly to ask her round for dinner after work.

'And to help me choose which ones to answer, Kelly. And by the way—thanks for your letter! That was a sweet thought.'

'My pleasure. Okay, I'll be at your place around seven. Shall I bring Paul?'

'Naturally,' smiled Storm—and had three bowls of minestrone steaming on the table when Paul and Kelly arrived.

After dinner, they sorted through Storm's letters together. Paul immediately discarded two more of the remaining selection, shaking his head sceptically over the obscure financial proposition involving 'only a very small investment, dear lady', and the invitation from

Mustapha Freedom. They arranged the offers in order
of preference—a preference largely determined by Paul
who (with those assessing blue eyes and that ready male
confidence about other people's lives) was soon in com-
mand. First of all they put the offer of a governess's job
for the summer in the U.S.A. Next the offer from the
big Birmingham hotel, who wanted someone to act as
manager ('which means caretaker', Storm had snorted)
for a series of commercial art exhibitions they were plan-
ning to hold. Then came the opal-hunting lady. Then
the satirical magazine ('sounds like some childish student
venture,' judged Paul coldly, a year out of medical
school) and the three unspecified jobs in foreign countries, which would have to be checked out before more
could be said about them. Last of all came the balloon
race.

'We won't actually chuck it out yet,' said Paul, 'because one never knows—but you won't seriously be
considering that one, Storm.'

'No,' said Storm, her green eyes thoughtful, 'not
seriously.'

'After all,' said Kelly, glancing at Storm's pretty face
with a hint of anxiety, 'a balloon race isn't going to pay
the rent, is it?'

'No,' said Storm decisively. 'Of course it isn't. More
coffee?'

On their way home later on, Kelly turned to Paul with
a rueful face.

'I wish you hadn't put that balloon business last,
darling,' she said.

Paul's eyebrows lifted as he changed gear, 'Why not?
It was the least sensible of them all.'

'Of course it was,' agreed Kelly. 'Which is why you

should have put it second last—or even top of the list.'

'You mean—to steer Storm away from it?'

'Yes,' said Kelly, leaning her shiny brown head against Paul's arm.

Paul sighed. 'I don't think I'll ever understand women,' he said.

'Well, it takes a long time to understand Storm Calderwood, anyway,' said Kelly thoughtfully. 'She'll be off to see the balloon man first thing to-morrow. You'll see.'

Storm checked herself in the mirror. White skirt, dark green cotton jacket, bare golden legs and white canvas shoes—it was a sporty little ensemble, showing her figure off well. She tied her hair back, slid on her prettiest pair of dark glasses as a concession to the October morning sun, and stepped outside with her big straw basket.

She glanced at the address on the letter—24 Whitethorn Road. Not exactly London's most prepossessing address, reflected Storm. It was the dockland, near the Isle of Dogs. Part of the East End of the city that had been so badly blitzed in the last war. And apart from that rather off-putting address, all she had to go on was a name—Jason Bentley. Definitely an upper-class name, she thought, reading through the terse little note:

Dear Virtuous Lady,
I need a partner for a European balloon race—not necessarily virtuous, just female. Interested? Fitness and a head for heights essential. Call round any morning before the end of the month.

The name was signed neatly, with no arrogance in the form of flourishes or scrolls. A hard, neat, clear note.

She had to take two buses to get to Whitethorn Road, and found herself wondering why she had chosen—against all logic—to try the balloon man first. And she had plenty of time to answer her own question, because the first number she came across in Whitethorn Road was 2301—only 2277 to go. Natural perversity, she supposed. Because it was what other people—especially Paul Phillips, with his rather pedantic voice—had expected her to do. And also because she rather liked the cool, hard tone of Jason Bentley's note. There was nothing sentimental or clever about it—it was plain and uncompromising. Even though the idea of a balloon race (and Storm realised that she had never even seen a balloon yet) was about the most wildly impractical thing she had ever heard. In fact, that combination of hard clarity and impractical adventure exactly suited her mood right now. Governessing in America? After that little tiger Majeed? No, thank you!

Whitethorn Road was long, dirty, and in need of repair. It consisted of huge warehouses, most crumbling, some smallish factories, grimy-looking pubs and flats, garages and workshops. Behind the Victorian brickwork, the skyline was dominated by the hulking shapes of cranes and the five huge steel puddings of a gasworks. Beyond were the dirty funnels of various dirty ships on the river. The air was busy with sirens and engines, and a pair of oil-covered men who passed by her whistled at her legs with a piercing industrial enthusiasm that was quite deafening. She was beginning to regret having ever left her flat by the time she reached the other end of Whitethorn Road, where the warehouses were even more crumbly and rickety, and the factories were starting to give way to large derelict plots, waist-high in rubble and weeds, beyond which could be seen the glinting sweep of the river and a congregation of blackish barges. There was an unexpectedly large and rusty boat, propped up on baulks of timber, a used car lot populated by two yapping mongrels and a few dozen extremely used cars—and then a long warehouse, upon whose blistered wooden doors was painted the number 24.

Storm paused dubiously. This didn't look like the beginning of anything promising at all. Although there was a bright red Lamborghini parked across the street, a deliciously glamorous and elegant-looking car. If you were flighty, that is, and easily impressed by that sort of male exhibitionism. Storm glared at the wicked thing, grateful for the fact that she was above such follies, and pushed the big timber door of the warehouse open.

The long, echoing building was cool and dimly lit. Six skylights in the roof sent shafts of sunlight through the dusty air to splash against the walls and floor—where a man was working on something amid a vast expanse of crimson and turquoise material. He turned as she walked towards him, a startlingly masculine figure, dressed only in faded jeans that hugged his slim hips, and a pair of track shoes. His powerful, lean torso was naked, and the sleek muscles of his arms and shoulders were tracked with sweat and stippled with sawdust.

'Mr Bentley?' Storm asked hesitantly. The eyes that met hers with a shocking directness were an imperious hazel-green, flecked with fierce glints of gold.

'That's right,' he nodded. 'Are you the Virtuous Lady?'

'Yes.'

She studied him quickly as he came over to her. Dust lay in the crisp curls that covered his broad chest, and in his dark hair. This almost savage figure was a far cry from the suave image she had expected. This man's glittering eyes and commanding bearing were slightly intimidating. And no amount of sophisticated veneer, she reflected, would be able to quite conceal the naked, unmistakably male power of this man. It was a quality that underlay the severe, cold beauty of his features.

'Well, you look fit enough,' he said calmly, giving her an unashamed up-and-down stare.

'Oh?' she said, taken aback.

'Are you really twenty-two?' he asked bluntly. 'You look about eighteen.'

'I'm twenty-two all right,' she said, nettled at his directness.

'It doesn't matter anyhow,' he said, and smiled. He really was an extraordinarily handsome man, she realised, beginning to feel slightly flustered by his cool, penetrating stare.

'Thank you for answering my advertisement,' she said coolly, trying to recover her poise.

'Thank you for coming,' he nodded. 'And I can assure you that what I have in mind is neither illegal nor boring.' He turned to pull on a T-shirt, and she watched the rippling muscles disappear under the cool white cotton. 'My last crew-member had to drop out in a hurry,' he said as his tousled head emerged.

'Not literally, I hope?' she smiled.

'Not quite,' he said drily. 'She changed her mind. It's a woman's prerogative, I understand.' He surveyed her with speculative eyes. 'Ever done any flying?'

'Only in airplanes,' she confessed.

'Well, ballooning's different,' he warned her, his tawny eyes bright, and then waved at the silky swath of bright material across the floor. 'There she is, Virtuous Lady—my pride and joy.'

'Oh.' Storm surveyed the sheet of colour dubiously, trying to find something complimentary to say. Jason Bentley pulled on a suede jacket, suddenly transforming himself into a figure of almost piratical elegance, and picked up wallet and car-keys from a chair.

'Shall we go for a drink somewhere and talk things over?'

'Why not?' She followed him to the door, studying him sideways as she went. A graceful man, who moved with the sure precision of a big cat. A commanding man, not at all the type you'd expect to find gallivanting around in balloons. Although she didn't really know what she had expected. Anyway, this man looked hard and efficient and successful. And very sexy. If you cared about things like that. As he opened the door of the red Lamborghini, she smiled to herself. It was the perfect car for him, hard and masculine and efficient. As she buckled her safety-belt, she glanced up at the warehouse.

'This isn't quite what *I* expected,' she said.

He smiled, switching on the engine.

'Balloons are fairly substantial things, even when they're deflated. There's not much room for it in my flat, so I rent this place from a friend in the shipping trade.'

'You aren't—er—a professional balloonist?' she asked as he drove past the huge steel legs of half a dozen mobile cranes.

'Hardly,' he said drily. 'Ballooning doesn't make money, it burns it up.'

'Though I take it there's a substantial prize attached to this race of yours?' she asked gently.

He glanced at her, tawny eyes amused.

'You're very sharp, Virtuous Lady. Yes, there's a first prize of twenty thousand pounds. Second prize eight thousand. And a further five thousand to be divided among the remaining people in the top ten.'

Storm looked at the slim gold watch on the strong wrist, at the leather-panelled dashboard of the beautiful car.

'I had no idea,' she murmured. 'That sounds an awful lot of money, Mr Bentley.'

'It's the biggest prize ever offered for a balloon race.' His voice, she noticed, was deep and vibrant. 'Besides which,' he added, pulling up outside a nautical-looking pub overlooking the docks, 'my balloon will be carrying a large yellow advertisement for a well-known Italian vermouth.'

'Are they sponsoring you?'

'They're meeting almost all the costs,' he nodded, switching off the discreet thunder of the engine. Storm did not open her own door, guessing instinctively that he would prefer to let her out himself. Jason Bentley had a lot of style, she was beginning to discover.

'It offends my aesthetic sense, of course,' he said, opening her door, 'but the vermouth people have been very generous.' He smiled, a tiger's smile that revealed perfect teeth and that carved fascinating clefts in the hard cheeks. He took her arm in a firm grasp and piloted her over to an umbrella-covered table on the edge of the patio. All her life, Storm had been the kind of girl men turned to look at. It was a novel experience being with the kind of man girls turned to look at with that inane flutter of the lids that women seemed to think men found irresistible. Idiots! Jason Bentley eased her chair beneath her bottom with expert gallantry and sat down opposite her, a dashing figure straight out of some glamorous advertisement. But much harder and more ruthless-looking than that, once you looked carefully into the tawny eyes, and noted the determined set of the rather cruelly handsome mouth.

'Take your dark glasses off,' he invited, and she obeyed, dropping them into her big straw basket. He stared at her for a second.

'You really are very beautiful, Virtuous Lady,' he said calmly, and to her dismay, Storm felt the blood rise to her cheeks. But he seemed not to have noticed. 'This is very fortunate, dear lady. There are distinct possibilities in this.'

'Such as?' she asked coolly. A waiter had materialised, and Jason Bentley gave him their orders (shandy for Storm, who was intent upon her virtuous image, lager for him).

'Such as,' he said, examining her with a rather disquieting intentness, his eyes pausing with shameless flattery at her breasts and mouth, 'my beloved sponsors. Who are incapable of resisting a pretty face. Or a pair of pretty legs. Of which yours,' he grinned, 'are among the prettiest around.' The arrival of the waiter silenced the retort that had sprung to Storm's lips. She sipped at her shandy, watching him with cool eyes.

'What do my legs have to do with your sponsor, Mr Bentley?'

'I should think there'd be miles of good publicity to be made out of the image of a gorgeous blonde sailing through the clouds in a balloon,' he said calmly, putting his glass down. 'And that could mean a big fee for you—even a contract. My last partner wasn't bad-looking,' he said mildly, 'but she didn't have your style.'

'Oh,' said Storm, glaring at the busty brunette who was casting voluptuous smiles in Jason's direction. On principle, she resented any other women making eyes at the man she was with—even though she was above the petty jealousies that seemed to beset her sex when confronted with anything in trousers. She studied his face carefully, noting the lines of decision around the harsh, passionate mouth, the level, hard quality in the tawny eyes. Not a man to make an enemy of.

'What do you do when you're not ballooning, Mr Bentley?' she asked inconsequentially.

His eyes glinted.

'I'm a lawyer, Virtuous Lady. Or I was.'

'Have you been disbarred?' she asked with a hint of mockery, and instantly regretted it. There was a steely quality in those eyes that chilled her.

'No, I haven't been disbarred,' he said coolly, his lean brown fingers drumming on the table.

'I'm sorry, I didn't mean that to sound nasty,' she apologised. 'Why did you say "was", then? Couldn't I go to you if I got into trouble with the police?'

'You'd have to go through a solicitor,' he said drily, 'but yes—I was practising up to last fortnight. I've just decided to take a rest from the—er—scales of justice. And the sword.' He said this with such a bitter note in his voice that Storm blinked. There was something concealed here, some painful mystery which the cold, tawny eyes had already covered up.

'And what about you, Virtuous Lady? What do you do for a living?'

'You haven't even asked my name,' she said, watching him over the rim of her glass. The clefts appeared in his cheeks again, and the smile was ironic.

'As a successful lawyer,' he said, 'I soon learned that names were often totally unreliable—and often at the complete discretion of the client.'

'Meaning?'

'Meaning that you'd give me your name—or someone else's name—when you felt like it.' The cool, sharp tone stung her for some reason.

'I'm no criminal, Mr Bentley—and I wouldn't give you a false name.'

'Naturally,' he purred, his smile mocking, 'you're a Virtuous Lady, and above suspicion. I simply have a naturally cynical cast of mind.'

'My name is Storm Calderwood, Mr Bentley,' she said, her voice cold. 'And the last job I had was as a governess to the son of an Arabian sheik.'

'Storm,' he said, his beautiful eyes mocking now, 'what a perfect name for you. Why were you called that?'

'It was my father's idea,' she said, flushing a little. Her name had often been a source of discomfort to her. 'I was born at sea—on a liner. My mother had me in her cabin, during a big storm. My father always claimed that it was the storm that brought me on, because I was six weeks premature. I should really have been born in London, long after we'd got back from America.' She sipped her shandy, very much aware of the male eyes that were watching her intently. 'But there it is. It's a silly name.'

'On the contrary,' he said seriously, 'it's a remarkably beautiful name—for a remarkably beautiful young

lady.' His fingers were drumming on the table. 'Besides
which, the sponsors will love it.' He was watching her
with the cool approval of a trainer looking over a
racehorse he was intending to buy. A spurt of resent-
ment went through her, but she bit it down. She was
going to be cool and hard—just as cool and hard as Jason
Bentley!

'You're very confident that I'm going to join you, Mr
Bentley,' she said drily.

'My name is Jason,' he smiled. 'May I call you Storm?'

'Do.' She dropped her eyes, wondering why on earth
he should be able to make her tummy jump in that way,
simply by smiling into her eyes.

'Well, I very much hope you'll join me,' he said. He
turned in his chair and looked out over the throbbing
dockland. Storm examined his hard, clean profile, and
wondered whether she liked him or not.

'I'm longing to get away from all this,' he muttered,
almost to himself. 'Away from all the bustle and noise,
all the sordidness and cruelty.'

'If you don't like sordidness and cruelty,' she retorted
mildly, 'you shouldn't have become a lawyer.'

Tawny eyes found hers icily, filled with a hard challenge that sent a cold trickle down her spine.

'That's right, Virtuous Lady,' he said softly, his face
bitter again, 'I shouldn't have become a lawyer.'

A flight of gulls drifted screaming across the umbrel-
laed tables of the little patio, and a distant tug whooped.
Storm shifted uncomfortably. There was something
piercing in this man's eyes, a hard quality about him that
threatened and chilled. She was beginning to feel that
she didn't like him, after all.

'Tell me about your race,' she invited.

'Ah—the race.' He sat back in his chair, clasped his hands behind his neck, and favoured her with one of his stomach-jolting smiles. Really, Storm thought, he was capable of having the most diverse effects on you. 'It isn't particularly long,' he said, 'about two hundred miles—with as many or as few stops as the competitors want. It's really the last race of the season—the Italians call it La Corsa delle Foglie Cadenti—the Race of the Falling Leaves.'

'That's a pretty name,' she smiled.

'The Italians are a sentimental race,' he said drily, and her smile evaporated. 'It takes place on the fifth of next month. From Cremona in Italy to Konstanz in Switzerland.'

Storm blinked. 'But that's right across the Alps!'

'Indeed,' he nodded with a slight smile. 'The official name is the Trans-Alps Balloon Race.'

She stared at him, watching the slow smile on the curve of the disturbingly cruel lips, the sparkle in the green depths of his eyes.

'Mr Bentley—Jason—how high are the Alps?'

'Where we'll cross them? Not more than ten or eleven thousand feet.'

'*Eleven thousand feet?*' She gaped. 'And how high do balloons go?'

'In this instance, about thirteen thousand feet.' He finished off his lager calmly and watched her.

'B-but—' She paused for breath. 'That's as high as planes fly!'

He shrugged. 'It's not nearly as high as some planes fly. Naturally, it will be extremely cold. And you'll probably feel the altitude in various ways. But don't forget that the Alps will be the highest part of the race by far—and there'll only be about seventy miles of them.'

'Seventy miles sounds an awful long way,' she said. There was an uneasy feeling in the pit of her stomach, a tension that was part fear and part excitement.

Jason took a gold Parker out of his pocket, and unfolded a little notebook.

'Shall we get down to brass tacks, Storm?'

'All right.'

'Okay.' He made notes on the pad as he talked, quickly and neatly, allowing Storm to admire strong, elegant hands that might have belonged to a master musician. 'In the first place, I'll try and persuade the sponsors to pay you a reasonable salary from now until the end of the race. Plus your fares to and from the race itself. And to give you some kind of advertising contract. Which will mean showing your pretty legs off here and there, maybe one or two interviews in magazines. Perhaps even on TV.'

She stared at him, not knowing whether to be offended or pleased at his cool, professional tone.

'If that falls through, I'll pay your fares and salary myself—to be negotiated to our mutual satisfaction. Right?'

She nodded, beginning to feel that Jason Bentley was probably a very good lawyer indeed—there was an authority, a cold efficiency, about him that tended to flatten all opposition.

'Secondly. You'll get one-third of all prize money we win. That could be as much as six thousand pounds—or as little as nothing. I intend to win, naturally—but I can't guarantee that. Three—I'll pay comprehensive life and accident insurance on you for the whole duration of the exercise. You name the beneficiary. And I'll undertake to pay for any medical treatment you might need for any reason during the period we're in Europe.' He signalled to the waiter for a repeat round, then glanced up at her with keen eyes. 'Fourthly—I'll undertake to pay for all clothing and gear you'll need for the race. That includes any fashion clothes you want. And a gown for the ball.'

'The ball?'

'Well, there are two of them, actually.' He grimaced. 'It's part of the publicity programme for the race. The whole thing is really designed to publicise ballooning as a sport. Yes, there's a dance in Cremona on the night before the race. Which will be rather,' he smiled rather grimly, 'like the dance before the battle of Waterloo. And at the end of the race, in Konstanz—that's Constance in English—there's a fancy-dress ball for the survivors.' Storm's green eyes lit up, and he surveyed her with dry irony. 'You'll also be expected to dress beautifully throughout, Virtuous Lady. In fact, you could get us disqualified if you're not immaculately turned out. The sponsors of the race want this to be as glamorous a performance as possible.'

'I take it that side of things doesn't interest you?' she enquired, accepting her shandy from the waiter.

He shrugged again.

'I'm interested in the twenty thousand pounds. And in ballooning. And perhaps most of all,' he grinned, a tawny light in his eyes, 'in competing.' He pulled the page out of his notepad, folded it, and passed it to her. 'I've written it all down there, Storm. With my phone number. Think it over—and then ring me when you've made your mind up. But please don't take too long about it.' He drank from his glass, watching her carefully. 'There's not much time—and a lot of shopping to do. Not to mention the need for some practice.'

'Practice?'

'At ballooning. If we're to travel two hundred miles across the Alps together, you'd better know something about balloons—even though you'll only be a bit of decoration.'

'Decoration?' she snapped. The cool, dismissive way he had said it stung her. He smiled somewhat mockingly.

'Ornamentation, then, if you prefer it. Your function is simply to look glamorous and feminine, Storm. And to drape yourself beautifully over me whenever we're within range of cameras or spectators.'

'I'm not sure I like the sound of that,' she said angrily.

The harsh, beautiful mouth smiled bitterly.

'That's the deal, Virtuous Lady. The funds for this race are put up by the Balloonists' Association, various manufacturers of sporting equipment—and the people who make and design the balloons themselves. They make the rules. And this race draws a hell of a lot of publicity, even though it's only four years old. Personally, I find the idea of so-called glamorous females swooning everywhere as distasteful as you do. There's a lot of razzmatazz attached, as you'll find. But there it is, like it or lump it. If you don't like the idea, Storm, I'm going to have to find a professional model. Or even drag one of my cousins into it—God forbid.' He drummed his fingers on the table again, smiling coldly at her. 'Have you any questions of your own?'

'You know very little about me, Jason—'

'I don't wish to know anything about you,' he interrupted drily. 'This will be a business partnership, despite all the razzmatazz and flummery. Get that into your blonde head right away. And I don't expect you to want to know *my* life history, either.'

She stared at him angrily, stung once again by the implied snub in his cold tone.

'You're very abrupt,' she complained.

'I'm a lawyer,' he shrugged, his eyes suddenly hard.

'Well, there's one question I want to ask, Mr Lawyer,' she said sharply. 'You don't look very poor to me. And that passion wagon—' she pointed to the red Lamborghini in the dirty street below, '—that didn't come cheap.'

'So?' he asked flatly.

'So—you're successful, right?'

'Very,' he agreed with frigid arrogance, his eyes challenging hers stonily.

'Then how does a highly successful lawyer get to take an autumn holiday ballooning around the Alps? Isn't this your busiest period right now?'

Once again, there was a glacial anger in the hazel eyes, and the cruelty of the passionate mouth deepened. She noticed that the muscles under his T-shirt were tense.

'That's my business,' he said in a harsh voice. 'But if you must know, I happen to need a break. I want to get out of this damned city and its messy lives.'

'Do you mean—resign from the Bar?'

'That has nothing to do with you,' he snapped. There was real anger in the splendid face now. 'If you want to check my credentials, contact the Secretary of the Law Association. Otherwise, Virtuous Lady—don't probe. After all, I haven't asked why you were sacked from your last job, have I. It's none of my business—and this is a business-only arrangement. Let's be business partners, nothing more. Right?' He looked at his watch, then rose with the lithe power that was characteristic of the man. 'I have appointments to keep,' he said. 'Can I drop you anywhere?'

'Near any tube station,' she replied, rising unwillingly. 'Very well, Mr Bentley—I'm not going to probe into your private life—as you say, it's nothing to me anyway. I'll think over what you've said. And I'll ring you as soon as I've got the answer.' But don't count on it, she added silently. Don't count on it, Mr Cold-Eyes Lawyer.

As they were walking down to the car, they bumped into a couple coming up to the patio. Jason glanced at the girl, a pretty blonde with a lot of make-up carefully applied.

'Hullo, Tessa,' he smiled, putting out his hand.

The blonde woman beamed.

'Hi, Alex,' she chirped, putting out her hand to take his; but her partner, a tight-lipped little man in an expensive suit, whispered something in her ear, and hurried her past. Jason turned to stare after them, his hazel eyes hard and angry.

'What was that all about?' Storm wanted to know. 'You're not infectious, are you?'

He turned bitter eyes on her.

'I thought you were going to mind your own damned business?' he snapped. She quailed a little before his obvious anger, looked back at the couple, who were hurrying away, and then shrugged.

'It's none of my business,' she admitted quietly.

He pulled the door of the red sports car open for her.

*

'Jason Bentley?' The Law Association spokesman had a plummy, port-and-cigars sort of voice. 'He took silk four years ago, Miss—ah—'

'Calderwood. So there's nothing irregular about him?'

'I don't know what you mean by *irregular*, Miss Calderwood,' said the official frigidly. 'Mr Bentley happens to be one of our most talented and respected young criminal lawyers.'

'I see,' she said slowly. 'Do you know whether he's still practising?'

'You don't—ah—move in legal circles, I take it?' said port-and-cigars condescendingly. 'No? Well, Jason Bentley has had a rather spectacular run of successes lately. You might have read about one or two of them. Schabram twins? The Lord Ellbeck fraud case? Morgan and Outram?'

'Morgan and Outram sounds familiar,' she admitted. 'Weren't they the two thugs who murdered the policeman?'

'*Miss Calderwood*,' exclaimed port-and-cigars in a tone of outraged horror, 'Morgan and Outram were *acquitted* of the charges against them!'

'Oh. Thanks to Mr Bentley, I take it?'

'It was a brilliant defence,' said port-and-cigars, still unforgiving. 'The jury's verdict went right across the judge's summing up.'

'You mean Jason Bentley persuaded them to acquit Morgan and Whatsisname even though the judge had told them to convict?'

'To put it *horribly* crudely,' said the plummy voice coldly, 'yes. Is there anything else I can help you with, Miss—ah—?'

'And you say Jason Bentley specialises in getting crooks off?'

The temperature of the official's tone dropped to an all-time low.

'Mr Bentley has been extremely successful with his *clients*, Miss—ah—This may come as a surprise to you, but under English law, people are presumed innocent until proven guilty. When they are acquitted, Miss—ah—er—they are thus *de facto* presumed innocent. Indeed, they are *proved* innocent. And people who go around calling them *crooks*—' (He said the word as though it were unspeakably dirty) '—are liable to prosecution for slander.'

'I see. Well, thank you, Mr—ah—'

She rang off. So! Jason Bentley was a criminal lawyer. Someone who specialised in getting thugs off the hook, no matter how guilty they were. She recalled the Morgan and Outram case more clearly. They had been two gangland bully-boys who had shot a policeman while robbing a bank. That was the charge, anyway. Though everyone had known they were guilty. She had noticed the case in the papers just after her return from the Middle East, and had simply assumed that Morgan and Outram had been convicted. But they had got off. Scot-free. Thanks to Mr Jason Bentley, Q.C. Storm's lips curled in scorn. No doubt he would want to get away from the sordidness and cruelty! Jason Bentley was one of those men who used their clever minds to outwit the law, to allow murderers and thugs to escape the justice they so richly deserved. Picking up a nice fat fee on the way. She thought of the red sports car, the slim gold watch on the lean wrist. All paid for by grateful criminals. With money that was bloodstained and corrupt.

Sordidness and cruelty indeed!

Storm went into her tiny kitchen to make coffee. She knew a lot more about Jason Bentley now. All she needed to know. The cruel eyes, the cold, passionate curve of the mouth—were all explained now. An icy, clever man, who didn't need feelings or emotions. A man who had mastered the law in order to thwart it. An officer of justice who moved among criminals and murderers. Who made so much money that he could afford to go balloon racing across the Alps. Well, she had made up her mind about Jason Bentley, she decided, as she curled up with her coffee. She didn't like him one little bit—either him or his hypocritical profession. How would that policeman's widow have felt when she heard that her husband's murderers were being released, smiling and scot-free?

And was she, Storm Calderwood, going to be able to stomach close contact with Jason Bentley for the next month? She brooded over her coffee, green eyes thoughtful.

CHAPTER THREE

KELLY Oates looked at her fiancé with worried brown eyes, then glanced back at Storm.

'I had a hunch you'd go for the balloon race,' she said ruefully. 'And—now that you've found out he's a brilliant defence lawyer—what are you going to do?'

They were sitting in the tea-lounge at the St Clement's Hotel over cream scones. Across the table from Storm was the disapproving medical face of Paul Phillips. They had been accompanied by Steve Manning, one of Storm's friends, a boyish, smiling man with bright, amused blue eyes.

Storm brushed crumbs off her fingertips.

'Well,' she smiled, 'I think I'm going to accept.'

'Accept?' snapped Paul. 'Don't be foolish, Storm!'

'Storm,' said Kelly gently, 'I thought you said you didn't like the man at all?'

'I don't,' she said calmly. 'But I don't dislike him that much either. He's cold and hard and efficient—and that suits me.'

Paul snorted irritably. 'Is that because you imagine that *you're* cold and hard and efficient, by any chance?'

'In some ways I am,' she shrugged. 'I reckon I can handle myself.'

'You do realise that this—this—' Paul searched for a word, 'this *escapade* won't bring you a penny?'

'It could bring me six and a half thousand pounds,' corrected Storm gently.

'*If* you win,' Kelly pointed out.

'I happen to think Jason Bentley is very likely to win,' said Storm, sipping tea.

Steve Manning rubbed a brown cheek thoughtfully.

'Excuse me for butting in,' he said, 'but do you happen to know anything about balloons?'

'Not really,' Storm admitted, tossing her golden hair back. 'But it sounds delightful.'

'Hmmm,' said Steve. 'I've done a lot of flying—in light aircraft—and I can tell you that being up in the air is not to everyone's taste. I presume these aren't dirigible balloons?'

'What does that mean?'

'They don't have propellers—you can't steer them. Is that right?'

'I suppose not,' she agreed dubiously.

'So you could end up on the top of Mont Blanc,' pursued Steve, 'or in the Adriatic?'

'Look, Storm,' said Paul persuasively, 'that governess's job in America was very well paid. And they agreed to pay your fare to and from—'

'I happen to like the sound of a trans-Alpine balloon journey,' said Storm firmly. 'And if that means going with Jason Bentley, then I'll go with him. I've never done anything like this before—and if I don't go now, I probably never will. It's an adventure,' she explained, looking round at them with bright green eyes. 'Can't you see? It may not bring much money in the end—and the company could be a lot better—but it'll be something to remember.'

'I'll say it will,' said Paul darkly. 'Especially if you fall out over Chamonix. Or run out of hot air over a lake.'

'Storm,' pleaded Kelly, 'listen to us! How are you

going to keep paying the rent on your flat, for one thing?'

'Two hundred pounds came through from the Middle East this morning,' Storm replied. 'That'll cover the rent. And Jason—or his sponsors—will pay for all my gear. I'll look for a job when I get back from Switzerland.'

'*If* you get back from Switzerland,' snapped Paul. 'By which time you'll be flat broke, with no prospects—'

'I'm not a complete dimwit, Paul,' said Storm drily. 'I'll be able to write magazine articles about the journey. With my own pictures—I'm not a bad photographer. And the vermouth people might have more work for me.'

'Maybe. If. Perhaps.' Paul glared at her. 'You're being crazy, Storm—'

Kelly laid a quiet hand on Paul's arm, and he muttered himself into silence. Objecting, Kelly knew of old, would only strengthen Storm's obstinate will.

'Have some more tea,' she said diplomatically, pouring for them all. There was a rebellious glint in Storm's beautiful emerald eyes. 'Supposing you do go,' Kelly went on mildly, 'what exactly will you get out of it?'

'I told you—an adventure.'

'I'm inclined to agree,' said Steve Manning unexpectedly, and they all looked at him. 'Adventure happens to be a very important thing. If you miss out on it, you can never rest easy. You'll always regret it. No matter how silly the adventure seems to other people.' He smiled gently at them all. 'In my case it was free-fall parachuting. I was a para in the Army—in my younger days—and I took to free-fall stunts like a duck to water. Or I suppose I should say, like an eagle to the air.' He grinned. 'Well, I had to take longer and longer falls.

From higher and higher up. My girl-friend at the time—Les—used to get furious with me. She couldn't understand how I could take such stupid risks. Well, it was the adventure of it.' He drew a deep breath, suddenly aware that they were all staring at him. 'I didn't mean to make any speeches,' he said apologetically. 'But I think I understand what's on Storm's mind.' He munched a scone reflectively. 'Of course, I ended up with a broken arm in the end.'

'There you are,' said Paul triumphantly.

'But I don't regret it,' Steve concluded mildly. He met Storm's green eyes with a smile. 'I'm not going to dispense any advice,' he told her. 'But you have to run your own life. You can't let other people make your decisions for you.'

'Thank you for that profound philosophical comment,' said Paul with angry sarcasm, and once again Kelly laid a restraining hand on his arm.

'Steve's right, of course,' she said quietly. 'No one can make your decisions for you, Storm. You simply have to do what you think is right for yourself.'

And in fact, Storm's own feelings about the race—and Jason Bentley—were a lot less certain than she pretended. She wanted to go, she knew that. The idea of the race, of floating over the Alps, *was* enormously appealing. Even though she had no real idea what was involved. As for Jason, there was something about that very handsome, very arrogant face that haunted her. She didn't like him. And she didn't like the idea of the cold work he did. But he was, as she had told Kelly and the other two, efficient and dispassionate. He looked like the sort of person who got things done.

She was forced to admit to herself that she felt drawn to him partly because her own life was such a tangle at the moment. If the truth be known, she sighed to herself, her life had never gone straight since her parents' death. After the traumatic shock of losing them, she had never dared to take anything seriously. And the world had little place for dabblers—which was why her life, despite the advantages of brains and—she flattered herself—a little beauty, had always been slightly confused and unsatisfactory. Why she had never been able to settle to a job and a man, the way her friends had. And why she was so attracted to the paradox of Jason's rock-like stability and adventurous romance. She liked the idea of his clarity, his unemotional precision. In a way, he was even a sort of substitute for the father she had missed so badly—a powerful male presence, ready to make decisions, to take control. And she hated the idea of going straight back to work, back to some soul-destroying routine. Even back to looking after some rich man's children for him. Storm had always loved children; but that two-month stay with the little Princeling had unnerved her. After the disaster over the smack she had been whisked out of the Sheikdom so quickly that she had scarcely had time to gather her wits properly. She needed a break, time to consider things properly.

And maybe, as Kelly had advised, to sort her confused self out.

So, by the time she had arrived home after tea that evening, Storm's green eyes were cloudy with thought. All in all, there were lots of reasons why she was tempted to accept Jason Bentley's offer. Lots of reasons, all adding up to a decision, none of them really clear enough to put a finger on.

The fact that Jason Bentley was the most attractive man she had ever met—the fact that she could recall every muscle in that tanned torso—did not cross her mind as one of the reasons.

Not even when his deep answer on the telephone sent a quiver of excitement running through her veins.

'Jason? It's Storm Calderwood.'

'Hullo, Virtuous Lady,' he replied calmly. 'Have you made your mind up yet?'

'I—well, almost.'

'Almost yes or almost no?'

'Almost yes.'

'I see.' There was that mocking note in his voice again. 'It's Friday today, Storm. I'm going to take the balloon up to-morrow afternoon, over at my father's place in Kent.' He paused. 'Would you like to come and see how it's done? That might help you to make your mind up.'

'I suppose—' She stopped, her heart beating a little faster. 'Yes,' she said at last, 'yes—all right.'

'Excellent.' She could almost see the curve of his smile. 'I'll pick you up tomorrow at ten. And bring you back on Sunday evening. Is that all right?'

'You mean—spend the night with you?' she said gauchely.

'Not exactly *with* me,' he said drily. 'You'll be perfectly safe, I assure you.'

'I didn't mean—oh well, never mind. Yes, that'll be all right, I suppose.'

'I'm so glad to hear it,' he said with cool irony. 'Better bring something warm to wear. Oh, and where do you live?'

She told him, her mind beginning to race.

'Whereabouts is your father's place in Kent?' she asked.

'Sutton Valence. It's not very far from London—and quite civilised. Very well—tomorrow at ten.'

'Oh,' she said. The line purred in her ear.

Sutton Valence was set against rising ground, a lush English scene of pastureland and rolling meadows, majestic clumps of oaks and newly-sprouting elms, and a limitless, peaceful English sky. The Lamborghini had brought them from London with the muted thunder of its big exhausts, and as they breasted Colby Hill, Storm gazed across the idyllic countryside with a half-smile on her rebellious mouth.

'It's beautiful,' she sighed. 'I missed this so much out in the Middle East—all this greenery and peace. I don't know—nature seems gentler here.'

'Nature's never altogether gentle,' Jason said quietly. 'My father's farm is beyond the village, behind that long line of furze on the crest of that hill.'

'Where's the balloon, by the way?' she asked.

'The one I'm using for the race is still in Whitethorn Road. I'm working on the basket—the cabin. I've got another one at Netherby.'

'I'm quite looking forward to going up,' she said, looking at his profile. 'I just hope I can be helpful.'

Hazel eyes met hers for an instant, and the ironic smile was back, tugging those fascinating lines around the intriguing mouth.

'I've told you, Storm, you're just decoration. You'd better simply concentrate on not falling out, or getting airsick.'

'I'll do my best,' she said rather shortly. She was

resentful of that aspect of the trip. Why should she be simply 'decoration'? The beautiful, rolling countryside spread out in front of them was inviting, a smiling landscape of rich fields and beautiful farmhouses. The big Jersey cattle in the green fields had the well fed, glossy look of animals that are kept as a wealthy man's hobby, rather than as money-making livestock. It occurred to Storm that this was no countryside for the un-moneyed. She glanced at Jason again.

'Is your father retired?' she prompted.

'Yes—much against his will. He was a judge. He's still a local magistrate, of course.'

'A judge? Did you ever have to defend a client in one of his cases?'

'No. That would have been very wrong.'

'Rather lucky,' she commented lightly, 'seeing that you would have been on opposite sides.'

'Why opposite sides?' he asked, looking at her sharply.

'Oh,' she said innocently, 'I thought counsel for the defence always tried to get the accused person out of the law's clutches.'

'That's a funny way of putting it,' he said stiffly. 'The point of a trial is to ascertain whether someone is guilty—not to punish him willy-nilly.'

'Don't be so pompous,' she laughed, fully aware that her tone had stung him.

'I'm sorry if that sounds pompous,' he retorted. 'It happens to be a principle enshrined in English law.'

'What—justice? Equity?'

'Something like that,' he said, his fierce eyes meeting hers again. 'Why sneer at it?'

'Well,' she said, with a touch of self-righteous indignation, 'I don't always call what lawyers achieve "justice", Jason. And nor would you, if you were being honest.'

The line of his mouth set hard, and Storm realised that she was treading on thin ice. There was a bitter, implacable look about him that it would not do to arouse.

'Tell me, Storm,' he said quietly, 'are you trying to get at something?'

'Well, yes—I am,' she said rashly. 'I think I know the reason why your last partner for the race changed her mind. And why that couple we met at the pub cut you dead. I've been hearing about your exploits lately. And, quite frankly, it made me sick.'

The brown hands on the steering wheel were suddenly white-knuckled with tension. She had scored, Storm gloated somewhat nervously, though his voice was still calm and even. 'Did it indeed? Would you care to elaborate?'

'If you really want me to,' she said, rubbing her suddenly sweaty palms on her jeans. 'A few weeks ago you defended a pair of heroes called Morgan and Outram. Am I right?'

'Yes,' he grated, fierce eyes fixed on the road ahead.

'And you got them off. They were supposed to have shot a young policeman in cold blood, weren't they? A colleague of yours told me all this very proudly, by the way. And you gave such a good performance that the jury acquitted them—even though the judge more or less ordered them to give a verdict of guilty.' She glanced at him, and saw with a thrill that his face was pale under the tan.

'Well?' he asked quietly.

'Well? Is that all you can say? You got those killers

off, Jason. Even though they deserved to rot in jail—you got them off. To kill again, maybe—'

The car shrieked to a halt, pitching her forward with pounding heart. Jason took her chin in a painfully strong grip, and turned her head so that he could stare into her eyes with a ferocious anger that terrified her.

'You stupid little child,' he said, his voice all the harsher for being quiet and deadly. 'What the hell do you know about it?'

'I know enough to be able to tell wrong from right,' she said apprehensively, her hands trembling.

'Brilliant,' he sneered bitterly. 'And you imagine you can parcel up the whole world with your crude little judgments, made out of ignorance and stupidity?'

Storm twisted her head away to stare out of the window.

'Bullying me won't make it any less true, and you know it,' she said, her voice unsteady. 'Those two killed that policeman and—'

'May I remind you,' he said icily, 'that a jury of twelve impartial adults decided that Morgan and Outram were innocent? And they had been listening to expert evidence for three days. Now you—a stupid little child— imagine you know better than they did!'

'I'm *not* a child,' she snapped. 'You persuaded that jury to acquit them, against all the evidence—'

'What the hell do you think I am?' he demanded fiercely. 'Some kind of black magician? Jurymen and women aren't the bloody fools you take them for, Storm. You don't seriously think I could have clouded their judgment, do you?'

'Why not? You're a brilliant lawyer, aren't you?' she sneered. 'One of the rising stars in the profession, isn't

that true? And you've got brains, looks, eloquence—
you could have done it. And you did. And you got a nice
big fee for doing it, too!'

In the silence, a truck passed them with a whoosh and
a shock-wave. Storm turned to face Jason. His magnificent face was pale, his eyes blazing; and that passionate
cruel-looking mouth was twisted as if in pain.

'I'm not doing a very good job of convincing you, am
I?' he asked tensely. 'It doesn't occur to you that Morgan
and Outram might have been innocent after all? That I
might have saved two blameless people from a lifetime
in jail for a crime they didn't commit?'

'Blameless? They were gangsters,' she jeered. 'The
only difference was that they were rich gangsters—and
able to afford the expert services of Jason Bentley,
Q.C.! Who so very cleverly got them off the hook!'

For a minute she expected to feel his hand crashing
across her cheek, and she shut her eyes. The blow did
not come. Instead, he let his breath out with an explosive
hiss. His voice was harsh, frightening.

'If I were you, Storm, I wouldn't go any further right
now. You came very close to making me lose my temper—and that wouldn't have been good for you.'

She met the blazing eyes as unflinchingly as she could.
'Then tell me one thing,' she said in a shaky voice. 'Do
you—in your heart of hearts—believe that Morgan and
Outram were innocent?'

He stared at her tensely. 'Before I answer that, will
you answer one question for me?'

'What is it?' she invited.

'Why did you put that advertisement in *The Times*?'

'Because I needed a job,' she retorted. 'I don't—'

'Why did you need a job?' he asked calmly, his eyes

still flickering with the bright flame of anger.

'That's a stupid question,' she snapped irritably.

'Answer it.'

'Because I was unemployed, that's why!'

'And why were you unemployed?' he asked with a quiet persistence that was beginning to unnerve her.

'Why? Because I'd left my last job, that's why—'

'You left it?' he queried, one eyebrow raised. 'I thought you were dismissed.'

'It was through no fault of my own,' she defended herself. 'I was in an impossible situation—'

'Impossible?' he sneered at her. 'I don't think you can imagine what it's like to be really under pressure, Storm.' His cold eyes bored into her. 'You've got no idea at all. So—why were you sacked?'

'That's my business,' she retorted. 'Let's get back to Morgan and—'

'The truth is that you were sacked for beating a helpless child—isn't that so?' As she gaped at him, he repeated with frightening suddenness, '*Isn't that so?*'

'Yes,' she gasped, taken aback by the swiftness of his attack.

He smiled bitterly.

'Yes, that's the true story, isn't it? You were sacked for abusing a helpless little boy who couldn't defend himself—'

'*No!*'

'And who was in your charge, Storm. Handed over to your trust—your care.'

She stared at him, hypnotised. 'That was very moral, wasn't it? And you have the right to throw accusations around, do you?'

'Jason—' she said breathlessly, her face white, 'that's—who told you that? Miss Quinlan?'

'I've been researching *your* background too,' he told her with a dry smile. 'It's amazing what turns up, isn't it?'

'That's a lie,' she said, her voice trembling. 'If Miss Quinlan told you that, then she's—she's—'

'What?' he demanded shortly.

'It's a complete distortion of the truth,' she said, unaware of the tear that was glistening on her cheek. 'You don't even give me a chance to defend myself—'

'I'm not interested in your defence,' he retorted. 'No more than you were interested in mine a few minutes ago. We can all accuse one another, Storm. That's what the law does—it accuses. And it's very hard to answer any accusation—no matter how innocent you may happen to be. Which is why lawyers exist. Not to get the guilty off the hook, but to help discover the truth.'

She stared at him with trembling lips. 'I didn't beat that little boy—'

'I've told you,' he said, 'I'm not interested. I hear enough sordid stories in the course of my work. I'm sick and tired of them. You were sacked for beating the Prince—isn't that true?'

'No,' she wailed, 'it's not true—well, it is true, in a horrible sort of way—'

'Listen to me, Storm,' Jason said coldly, tilting her chin up with a strong brown hand and staring into her blurred eyes. 'We aren't here to question each other's moral philosophies. We're entering a race as business partners—and that may be a lot more serious an undertaking than you imagine. You've made me extremely angry once already this morning. Don't repeat the experiment. Understood?'

She stared at him miserably.

'Is that understood, Miss Calderwood?'

'Yes,' she sniffed angrily, hurt beyond her previous experience.

He nodded slightly, his own eyes still holding that cold fire. 'Then let's get on to Netherby Hall.'

'I want to go back to London,' she demanded, blowing her nose as he switched on the engine.

'Oh, shut up,' Jason said drily. 'I'm beginning to regret ever having answered that idiotic advertisement of yours. I might have known it wouldn't have come to any good.'

'I'm not going up in any balloon with you,' she said petulantly. 'Take me back, damn it!'

'You can take the train back if you're so desperate,' he snapped, changing gear with a snarl of the finely-tuned engine.

Storm stared at him through red-rimmed, bitterly angry eyes.

'You still haven't had the courage to answer *my* question,' she said, her voice low. 'Do you really believe that Morgan and Outram were innocent?'

The muscles on his jaw rippled. 'Innocent?' He stared at the road ahead with unseeing eyes. 'Neither one of them pulled the trigger of the gun that killed P.C. Davis, if that's what you mean.'

'I don't believe you,' she retorted, brushing her eyes with her wrists.

'God! You don't think I give a twopenny damn what *you* think, do you?' he answered furiously. 'Now shut up for the last few miles, for both our sakes!'

Storm sat in smouldering silence, pain and anger burning inside her. Who the hell did he think he was?

Some special being, who had the right to make moral
pronouncements on lesser humans? She shot an angry
glance at the powerful figure at the wheel, so perfectly dressed in his Fair Isle sweater and his cotton
shirt, open just enough to show the first crisp curls
on his broad chest. Just who the *hell* did he think he
was?

She didn't believe him about those two gangsters.
There was something—she couldn't put her finger on
it—something elusive which told her that he didn't
believe they were innocent. Despite his self-righteous
tone, he was deeply upset by her challenge. The pig! She
ground her teeth. Well, he had managed to pay her back
with that little piece of malice from Miss Quinlan. As a
good lawyer, he *would* know just how to turn evidence
upside down and make his own case look like driven
snow. As for Miss Quinlan—the malicious old so-and-
so—did she realise she could effectively destroy Storm's
future career prospects by spreading around the story
that she had beaten Majeed Hussein? If only they could
have seen the truth, seen the little devil butting her in the
stomach! She would like to have seen Miss Quinlan
coping with Majeed. Huh!

She stared at the splendid old farmhouse ahead with
cold green eyes.

'Is that your father's place?' she enquired, dying to get
out of the Lamborghini.

'Yes,' Jason said calmly. She glanced at the mag-
nificently handsome face, now quiet and watchful. This
weekend wasn't going to be any picnic—and that was for
sure!

A tall, distinguished-looking man with silver hair
emerged from one of the barns as they drove up, and

greeted them with a wave. As she and Jason climbed out of the Lamborghini, he came up, grey eyes bright with pleasure.

'Wonderful to see you, my boy,' he smiled as he and Jason shook hands warmly.

Jason turned to Storm.

'Storm Calderwood—this is my father, Judge Bentley.'

'So you're the intrepid young lady who'll be going up in Jason's contraption?' smiled the Judge, taking her hand.

'I haven't committed myself yet, Judge,' she said, immediately liking the clear-eyed old man with the features that were so unmistakably like his son's.

'Please—not Judge, my dear. Call me Lockwood—that's my name. May I call you Storm?'

'Of course,' she smiled. Jason was watching her with an ironic glint in his eyes. She glanced round the beautifully kept old English farm buildings and to the rambling farmhouse in the big garden beyond. 'What a lovely place this is!'

The Judge beamed at her. '*I* think so,' he said with such unabashed pride that she was quite charmed. He took her arm in his left and Jason's in his right, and walked them to the farmhouse.

'It was built by one of our remote ancestors,' he told her. 'It's Elizabethan, you know.' He smiled beneath his silver moustache and murmured into Storm's ear, 'Absolutely *packed* with ghosts, my dear!'

'Don't let my father lead you up the garden path with his wild tales of ghosts,' Jason cautioned, smiling fondly at the old man. 'He's got a very keen sense of history, has my dad.'

'Well, you wait and see,' said the Judge unrepentantly.

The front door was wide open, and they passed through a glassed-in porch full of flourishing pot-plants into a big, comfortable-looking living-room that was absolutely typical of an old Kentish farmhouse. Dominated by a vast fireplace with gleaming and ancient brass-knobbed fenders, the room was panelled on two sides with oak, its walls hung with beautiful old rural paintings—glossy horses, prize cattle, a spectacularly beautiful landscape that looked like a Constable, and various seventeenth- and eighteenth-century portraits. Storm looked around with delight, noting the comfort evident in the big chairs, the rack of shotguns in a locked cabinet, the flowers in every vase, clumsily but brightly arranged. She turned to the Judge, who was watching her reactions with a little smile.

'It's wonderful! Like something out of the last century!'

'It's my home,' he said simply, his cheeks bright with pride.

Jason pointed at the magnificent old mantelpiece.

'Those were my mother's,' he told her, and she went to examine the dozens of china ornaments that stood, spotless and orderly, on the big marble beam. They were all farm animals, some obviously extremely old. Many were Staffordshire, primitive and charming; others were unbelievably finely worked, the delicate products of Meissen and Dresden, priceless and exquisite. Storm touched them with wonder, realising the love that must have gone into the lifelong collection of these charming and rare pieces—plump cows with dainty little legs, shaggy Highland cattle, little round pigs and stamping shire-horses, a tiny flock of painted china sheep.

'If I didn't know any better,' she said, 'I'd say these belonged in a museum.'

Jason smiled drily and turned to his father.

'I'd better make a phone call, Dad. I'll tell Annie to make some tea on the way.'

As Jason walked out, the Judge ushered Storm into the most comfortable of the armchairs, and sat down opposite her, smiling with gentle charm.

'Storm is such a pretty name,' he said. 'Jason tells me you were born during a storm at sea.'

'Yes, I was,' she said, rather surprised that the cool and dispassionate Jason should have told his father any such details about her. She explained the story in greater detail.

'And where are your parents now?' he enquired.

'They died—about six years ago. A motor accident.'

'Ah,' said the Judge, obviously horrified at having brought up a painful subject, 'I'm so sorry, my dear—I didn't mean to trespass.'

'It's quite all right,' she smiled, liking him even better. He was a very distinguished-looking old man, upright and obviously very fit, with the perfect manners of a bygone generation. Jason would be like this in forty years' time, she reflected.

'And your wife?' she prompted gently.

'No longer with me,' he told her regretfully, his grey eyes quiet and sad. 'She died two years ago this Christmas.' This time it was Storm's turn to be sorry. He waved away her apologies genially, his eyes watching her with deceptive attention. 'Tell me, has Jason been making you cry?'

She looked at him quickly, then smiled slightly.

'Does it show?'

'I'm a judge,' he said simply. 'I know a little about human nature. Would it be an old man's inquistiveness to ask what it was about?'

She sighed. 'Well, I'm not really sure. I was very rude to Jason, I'm afraid.'

'About what?'

'About his work.' She met the mild old eyes remorsefully. 'It was unforgivable of me. I just mentioned one of Jason's recent cases—and I'm afraid I suggested he'd got two guilty men off the book.'

'Morgan and Outram?' asked the Judge quietly. She nodded, twisting her hands, and a troubled, tired look crossed the Judge's patrician face.

'That wasn't very tactful of you, my dear,' he said gently. 'I'm beginning to wish I'd never heard of Morgan or Outram.'

'So am I,' she said, remembering the icy fury in Jason's face. Lockwood Bentley looked at her with wise eyes.

'Storm, can I give you a little bit of advice? Don't bring up that case again. I can't speak for Jason—but I can tell you he won't want to discuss any of his cases out of context.'

'I understand,' she nodded.

'There's another thing,' he said, standing up as a plump, rosy-faced woman brought in a beautiful silver tray of tea and cake. 'Ah, Annie, my dear. This is Storm Calderwood. Storm—Annie White, our housekeeper. My right-hand woman, in fact,' he added, and the woman dropped a beaming curtsey, answering the Judge's smile, and scurried out. Lockwood Bentley poured tea with careful hands.

'You were saying?' prompted Storm.

'Yes—about the law in general. It's a funny business, I dare say, and it seems very topsy-turvy to people who aren't involved in it.' He passed her the bone china cup and a thick slice of nut cake. 'Annie baked that—it's delicious, you'll see. But the law,' he continued, his eyes calm and friendly, 'is a massive and wonderful institution. It dispenses justice, Storm. Not charity or kindness. Cold, hard justice. That's not something humans can always understand.'

'I think I know what you mean,' she said.

He nodded. 'Good. Now, no doubt you think me a charming old man?' His smile was irresistible.

'Well—' she said, smiling in return.

'Well, maybe I am. But don't forget that I was a judge in the days before capital punishment was abolished in this country. I've sentenced men to death, Storm.'

There was a silence. Storm watched him, suddenly fascinated. He smiled, drinking his tea with relish.

'They were very wicked men, my dear. They thoroughly deserved their sentences. They did things that would make you wake up at night screaming. And I've never had a moment's regret about any of them.'

'But—' she hesitated, 'the same people today—'

'Would go to jail for life. Yes. Whether that's any more humane a sentence or not is very hard to say. But that is the law. Not the decision of one person—but the collective decision of all the people, past and present. Administered by a few men and women, very highly trained, and always in the full public scrutiny.'

Storm nodded slowly. Lockwood Bentley met her eyes with his own intelligent gaze. 'Don't be harsh on Jason, my dear. He has enough troubles of his own.' He shook his head thoughtfully. 'Jason's lost a lot of friends over this case, Storm. Stupid people, who didn't even follow the details closely enough to know that he was right. People who jumped to conclusions.'

She looked guiltily away.

'Just like I did,' she said unhappily.

'Don't blame yourself,' he smiled. 'But I know that his current girl-friend was one of the people who snubbed him—and that hurt him badly.'

'The one who was going to join him on the race?' she ventured.

Lockwood Bentley nodded.

'Yes. Flighty creature—but Jason was very fond of her, I believe. Anyway,' he smiled confidentially, 'don't be too quick to condemn him. I think I hear him coming down the stairs now—'

And the door opened, letting in Jason, who smiled at them both.

'Getting to know each other?' he asked. Storm noticed that the air of tension which had hung over him in London was slowly slipping away out here in the country. She determined to make a new start with Jason—if he would let her. There was a lot more to this powerful, beautiful man than she had first been prepared to see.

Lockwood poured tea for his son, a smile tugging at his silver moustache.

'We've been discussing the legal profession,' he said.

Jason's lip curled as he sat down, crossing his legs. The relaxed expression faded swiftly, and he met Storm's eyes with a cold, forbidding glint.

'I see. Storm has very definite views on the legal profession,' he said shortly.

Lockwood glanced at the two of them, then passed Jason his teacup.

'She tells me you two had a little disagreement on the way down from London?' he prompted gently.

'Storm happens to be a very argumentative young woman,' Jason said drily, and Storm's eyes flashed. He smiled at her icily. 'People who are cursed with a quarrelsome disposition shouldn't start a fight without getting their facts right. It's a bad mistake, don't you think?'

'Certainly,' she retorted with frigid politeness. All her resolutions about starting afresh with Jason flew to the winds. 'But people who have a lot of control over other people's lives should have some sense of responsibility, don't you think?'

The passionate mouth had become a hard line.

'Ignorant little girls shouldn't try and be too clever,' he snapped.

Seething, Storm glared at him. Hateful man! The elderly Judge looked from his son to Storm in some dismay. The beautiful young lady Jason had brought home for the weekend was obviously full of spirit. And there was some deep quarrel between them, that was obvious. He sighed quietly to himself. Such a pity—she really did seem a very charming young woman!

CHAPTER FOUR

STORM watched the powerful muscles in Jason's arms absently. He was securing the nylon rigging with quick, sure movements, his tawny lion's eyes intent on the work. Sam White, Annie's husband, had driven out to the field with them, and Storm had been sitting sullenly on a tree-stump while he and Jason unloaded the balloon off the truck. It now lay across the soft grass of the meadow, a long sheet of yellow and blue polyurethane. She surveyed the basket with disfavour—it looked comfortable enough, like a huge old-fashioned picnic basket—but it was only about five feet tall. Wouldn't they fall out if the balloon swayed?

She glanced up at the sky, feeling a knot of tension building up in her stomach. At least it was a beautiful day. The skies vaulted blue over this field in Kent, and it was warm enough for them all to have stripped to T-shirts. Storm looked at Jason covertly. He was undeniably a splendid figure of a man, broad-shouldered and lithe. Storm had always imagined lawyers to be dry, bespectacled people with prosperous tummies and pale skins. This one wasn't. He was hard and fit and tanned a deep mahogany-gold, and the muscles under the thin material of his shirt pulsed with power.

Only a blind woman would have denied that he was physically stunning—a man to make any female heart skip a beat. Which just went, Storm decided, to show how deceptive appearances could be. Because apart from her physical attraction to Jason Bentley, she found him an utterly hateful man—hard, ruthless, and obviously filled with dislike for Storm. Since the strained lunch in the beautiful old dining-room (at which the poor Judge had presided anxiously, trying to make up for the lack of conversation) Jason had hardly spoken three words to her. And when their eyes had met, it had been with a mutual dislike that even Sam White had noticed.

Preparations were obviously nearly complete now, and Jason was rigging up the big methylated spirits burner at the neck of the balloon. Storm watched in some trepidation as the burner ignited with a roar, sending a big blade of violet flame into the open neck of the balloon, which was supported by a wire framework. She slipped off her stump and walked up to Jason, who was checking the contents of the wicker cabin.

'Is this safe?' she asked, gesturing at the burner. 'Won't the balloon catch fire?'

'It's non-flammable,' he told her shortly.

She turned to watch the balloon. It was already beginning to fill with the hot air, swelling and rising perceptibly. All of a sudden, the reality of what they were about to do dawned on her, and she felt herself go slightly paler. Jason's sharp eyes did not miss the change, and he gave her a sardonic glance.

'Changing your mind?'

'Not at all,' she said coolly, and turned away.

The huge balloon slowly lifted itself off the ground, the creases and folds of its skin filling out steadily. She watched in fascination as it swelled, a brilliantly-coloured sphere that grew steadily, billowing upwards. Its size startled her. She had imagined something fairly small; this was the size of a cottage, a vast, bright sphere that was filling the sky above them. The hot air continued to rush into the open neck.

For the first time, the meaning of it all was becoming clear to Storm—the fascination of these huge, fragile structures, fiercely lighter than air, capable of that universal dream of humans everywhere—flight! She watched Jason's face as he stared upwards. It was eager, joyful—the face of a man with a dream. She came closer to liking him then than she had from the very beginning. By now the balloon was nearly ready, a massive striped bubble that tugged at the earth in its eagerness to be off. Sam had secured the basket with ropes pegged into the ground, and now these were taut. The shiny surface of the balloon was taut, too. What an extraordinary sight this would be, Storm realised—this huge fairy structure glowing in a peaceful green Kentish field!

She turned to find Jason opening the wicker door of the little basket for her. Her heart suddenly thumping, she stepped inside, instantly aware of the powerful tugs of the balloon on the light structure. He secured the door carefully with thick leather straps. The burner was still roaring just over their heads, and Storm looked up into the mouth of the balloon. The violet fire stabbed up into the luminous cavern up above, and the great shining sphere of polyurethane curved up and outwards and away fifteen feet over their heads. The noise of the burner was loud enough to prevent conversation, and Jason was communicating with Sam by signals. With a final thumbs-up sign and a broad grin, Sam released the last umbilical cord that held them to the earth. Clutching the rim of the basket with unfeeling hands, Storm felt gravity suddenly give way. She gasped in terror and delight, her blood fizzing with excitement as though her veins were filled with champagne—and then they began to rise.

She gaped down at the field beneath them, receding as they rose swiftly. Jason's firm hands were at the controls of the burner, judging their ascent carefully. Sam's figure dwindled beneath them, until he was only a waving doll standing next to a toy truck in a counterpane-sized field. She turned, alive with excitement, to Jason. He pointed at the altimeter. They had climbed a thousand feet already! The wicker cabin swayed gently under her feet, and she twined her arm round one of the guy-ropes to stare down at the fields beneath them.

And then Jason cut off the burner, and there was silence. An unbelievable, peaceful, beautiful silence, disturbed only by the sound of the wind and the quiet creaking of the wickerwork. As if in a dream, Storm stared about her. In the silence, they were still rising steadily, leaving the green-and-brown earth behind them. She could see fields and meadows stretched out across the flat landscape beneath them. Away to the right, the little town of Sutton Valence with its church spires, set against its sheltering outcrop of high ground. To the left, the three aquamarine pools of a fish-farm, a little stream, the grey glint of a millpond. All in miniature, an exquisite, perfect world built to scale for a child's delight. Two thousand five hundred feet. The great blue and yellow dome above them was thrusting upwards into the sky, the hot air in it pulling them away from the green of Kent towards the sky above. Jason's magnificent face was smiling at her with dry amusement.

'Enjoying it?'

'It's—it's *fabulous*!' she breathed. 'It's like something out of the Arabian Nights! And it's so quiet—'

'Yes.' He glanced out over the world beneath them, one brown hand holding the rigging. 'That's why I love balloons—as opposed to helicopters or planes. They're so quiet, so peaceful.' They stared at one another, the quiet seeping into them. Jason checked the altimeter.

'Three thousand feet. It'll be getting cooler soon. Best pull on your sweater.'

The air was indeed becoming deliciously cool, and Storm tugged her pink jersey on, pulling her blonde hair out from beneath its collar. Jason was watching her with inscrutable eyes, and once again she felt that jolt to the solar plexus that his eyes sometimes gave her.

Probably just the altitude, she decided firmly, and looked out over the little world below. There was, indeed, more sky than earth around them now. The bright sphere hung in the blue sky like a jewel, seeming almost motionless. In fact, as Storm suddenly noticed, they were drifting steadily south-east. She turned to Jason, concerned.

'Is there—is there any way of steering this thing?'

'Not by any mechanical means,' he answered calmly, leaning against the wicker and surveying her with calm, beautiful eyes. 'There's no engine, if that's what you mean.'

She gulped. 'Then how—how do you know where we're going?'

'To some extent, that's always a bit of a mystery with balloons,' he said, his intriguing mouth curving into its wry smile. 'We can control our descent and rise easily enough—with the burner, and by releasing more air with this release-cord. Apart from that, we have to trust to the prevailing winds.'

'The winds? Are we just—*drifting*?'

'Not exactly,' he said, checking the altimeter again. 'Five thousand feet. We won't go much higher this time—I don't want to have you screaming or vomiting everywhere.'

She shot him an angry glance.

'I'll do my best,' she retorted. 'So—how do you know where we're going?'

'For one thing, I checked the winds out before we left. Obviously, you wouldn't try and go in the opposite direction to the prevailing breeze. In this case, we're moving towards Lympne—which is where I want to be.'

'Why?'

'Because there's an airfield there,' he answered, tugging at the rigging, 'because it's a pretty spot—but chiefly because Sam is rushing that way right now with the truck, intending to meet us there.'

'Oh,' she said. 'What if the wind changes?'

'You really are full of questions, aren't you?' he commented.

She made a face at him. 'It's a long way down,' she reminded him. 'I'd just like to know, that's all.'

'Well, the winds move in different directions at different altitudes—to put it very simply. We just have to find the correct level, that's all.'

'Oh,' said Storm again. The world drifted past underneath them, a succession of tree-lined fields. A grey and pink village, dominated by one steep spire, was coming up beneath their cage now.

'Pluckley,' he informed her. She glanced at Jason's bronzed face. The slight wind was blowing his thick, dark hair away from his face, and he was devastatingly attractive. Or he would be, she reminded herself firmly, if she weren't a long way above such follies. She settled down to enjoy the flight.

The big fire crackled quietly in the grate. The Judge had had it burning brightly for them on their return earlier in the evening, and now it had died down to a sea of bright embers that sputtered and hissed comfortably in the quiet of the house. The Judge had retired to bed soon after dinner, pleading tiredness. In reality, Storm was sure, he was hoping for some kind of reconciliation between his son and their visitor. She glanced across at Jason, who was gazing into the fire with absent eyes, lying back on the thick woollen rug before the grate. She herself was sitting with her knees drawn up under her chin, hugging her shins. The glow of the firelight played across Jason's face. It was so still and peaceful in the old house that Storm could hear the distant hoot of an owl somewhere, and the occasional bark of a dog, farmyards away across Kent.

The balloon flight had been wonderful, an experience beyond her wildest dreams. Up in the deep blue sky they had felt free, untrammelled by any earthly considerations. They had drifted on the wings of high winds, silent and calm, with all of South-East England spread out at their feet. Near Lympne they had met their first patches of cloud, soft white misty stuff that blew through their rigging silently, leaving a faint wetness behind, and had started the descent. As the big blue and yellow balloon had touched down, as gently as a feather landing, Sam had arrived, grinning and waving from the wheel of the farm truck. Dazed with the experience, Storm had helped the two men to load the deflated balloon back on to the truck, and had sat wedged between them, dreaming all the way back to Sutton Valence, her mind still full of the deep, upside-down ocean of the sky.

When she looked over at him again, Jason was watching her, the firelight turning his beautiful eyes into flickering gold. Why *did* he have that effect on her? His voice was calm and gentle.

'You enjoyed the flight this afternoon, didn't you?'

'I loved it,' she nodded, her hair glinting in the warm light. 'I had no idea it was going to be anything like that.'

Jason shrugged slightly. 'Some men play golf or take to boats for pleasure. I go ballooning.'

'It would be a wonderful way of relaxing,' she agreed, adding cautiously, 'especially with a job as nerve-racking as yours.'

'What do you know about it?' he retorted, his smile tense.

She clenched her teeth, determined not to be drawn by his aggression again.

'Jason, I've made up my mind about the race. I'd like to come, after all.' She dropped her eyes, looking sadly at the hot coals. 'Though I guess you don't want me any more.'

There was a silence. Then Jason shifted, still staring into the coals, and asked,

'Why? Why do you want to come?'

'Do I have to give a reason?' she enquired gently.

He smiled bitterly. 'I've seen the look in your eyes all day, Storm. You don't like me, do you?'

She paused, unhappy and uncertain.

'Well—you said earlier on that we should leave personal feelings out of this, Jason. Maybe that would be the best thing. I want to go on this race for my own reasons. Because I don't want to go straight back to work. Because I want the adventure. Because I happen to have just fallen in love with ballooning.'

'I see,' he said. She watched the fine muscles across his stomach tense under his thin shirt as he crossed his long legs casually. 'Those are as good reasons as any, I guess. I might as well admit that I don't particularly enjoy your company either.' Their eyes met, and then they both looked away. 'But the race is in less than ten days' time. Also, you'll be very useful to me.'

'I thought I was intended simply as decoration?' she asked drily.

He nodded. 'You are. It so happens that you're a particularly beautiful piece of decoration.'

'Oh, really,' she snapped, wondering why her heart had trembled at his words. Jason smiled ironically across at her, the firelight casting shadows into the curves at the corners of his mouth.

'I don't happen to find you attractive on a personal level,' he said calmly. 'You just fit the bill—blonde hair, green eyes, pretty face and figure—the sponsors are going to love it. Which means more sponsorship for my balloon.'

'Oh,' she said, hugging her knees tightly.

'Besides which,' he continued, 'the points for the Trans-Alps race are awarded on a complicated system which includes something called "style". Meaning the way the balloon looks, the way it moves, the rigging— and the pilots.'

'I see.'

'I think I can trust to your vanity,' Jason said drily, 'not to let us down. Especially when we get you a decent outfit for the race.' He leaned forward, the soft light playing on the muscles of his forearms as he stirred the fire with a poker, then sat back. He looked at her, his eyes hard and challenging.

'So. I need you—and you need me. Is it a deal?'

'Yes,' she said, after a second's hesitation. 'It's a deal.'

He put out his hand, and Storm shook it, feeling his strong fingers close over hers for an instant. The contact between their palms for some reason made her spine tingle, and she looked at him, torn between dislike and attraction.

'It's far too early to go to bed,' he commented, looking at his watch. 'That's the trouble with the country—the evenings are so peaceful that you get bored.'

'I'm not bored,' she volunteered.

'Well, I am. Do you play chess?'

'Not very well,' she said hesitantly. 'I won't give you much of a game.'

'It'll pass the time, anyway.' He rose, and pulled a low table and two chairs in front of the fire. The solitary standard lamp in the corner shone on the oak panels as he drew the heavy brocade curtains shut. 'We won't need this,' he said, switching it off. 'We'll be able to see by the light of the fire.'

The room was illuminated by the gentle orange glow of the fire, and Storm roused herself to sit on one of the chairs as Jason brought the chess-set over and began setting the pieces out. They were of red and white ivory, Indian, and obviously very old. Storm picked up one of the knights and examined the horse's delicately-carved face.

'Your mother's?' she asked. He nodded, holding out clenched fists for her to choose a colour. She chose red, and he twisted the board round.

They played in silence, each intent on their own

thoughts as they moved the pieces dreamily across the chequerboard.

'Your queen's in check,' he advised her, eyes absent, and she picked up the smooth piece, studying his face.

'Jason,' she said hesitantly, 'I know I'm completely out of line—but will you tell me about that case? Please?'

Instantly his eyes were wary, and she could almost see the tension settle on his shoulders.

'What for?' he demanded angrily.

'Because I can see it's haunting you,' she said quietly. 'So can your father. I know you don't like me—but at least I'm someone to talk to. Wouldn't it do you good to talk about it?'

'You're an amateur psychiatrist, are you?' he enquired with biting sarcasm. 'Or are you just looking for some cheap thrills out of someone else's tragedy?'

'That's not fair,' she snapped, plonking the chess piece down thoughtlessly on to the board. Jason glanced at it.

'Hmm. Not a bad move.' He studied the board with alert eyes, his mouth compressed. Despairing, Storm sat back. That mouth was so bone-meltingly attractive, she thought—it could make your heart jump when it smiled in a certain way. Yet it was hardly ever relaxed—always either compressed with tension or tugged into a bitter sneer. What *was* eating Jason Bentley? She took a deep breath, and tried again.

'Morgan and Outram—were they the only ones involved in the robbery?'

'For God's sake!' His head snapped up to stare at her furiously. 'What the hell are you asking for? Can't you leave it alone?'

'I could if you could,' she answered quietly.

He stared at her for a second longer, then slumped back in his chair.

'Morgan and Outram,' he said slowly, his eyes losing their focus. 'A lawyer is sheltered from his cases, you know. He never sees his clients alone. There's always at least a solicitor present. Sometimes guards, policemen, legal officials of every kind.' He leaned forward, moving a piece, and stared at her angrily. 'It's your move,' he told her, and Storm dropped her eyes to the board, pretending to concentrate.

'You want to know about Morgan and Outram? Two frightened kids, that's all. Nasty kids, admittedly, kids who'd gone wrong. But just kids, all the same. Billy Morgan was eighteen, Butch Outram nineteen. They were a couple of skinny, white-faced boys who'd got mixed up in a crowd of ugly swine—one of the East End's nastiest gangs. And the charge was nasty, too. P.C. Davis wasn't much older than Morgan or Outram. He'd come to investigate some fuss at the bank in Cannon Street. As he walked through the door, five men in stocking masks ran past him. One of them shot him—and he was dead by the time the ambulance came. Later that same day, the police picked up Morgan and Outram with some of the stolen money. And the gun that killed the policeman.'

Storm was no longer watching the board, but was staring at his face, hanging on his words.

'So, naturally, they were charged. The *prima facie* evidence was very powerful. Circumstantial—but the good, solid stuff that successful prosecutions are built on—the money, the murder weapon, two kids who'd been thrown on the scrap-heap, and who'd retaliated against a society they hated and feared. It's still your move.'

She looked blindly at the board, pushed a piece into place, then looked up at Jason again. He considered her move, as though utterly relaxed; but Storm could tell, with a woman's quick instinct, that every muscle in the powerful torso was strained and teased.

'But they weren't guilty?' she prompted quietly.

'They weren't guilty as charged, no. I know that neither of them was near Cannon Street when the shooting took place.'

'But the money? The gun?'

'They were part of the gang, all right. And the clever boys had planted all the evidence on these two young idiots.' He moved another piece. 'That's check, by the way.'

Storm was past caring about the game.

'What happened then?' she demanded.

'Well, bad as things looked against these two young thugs, they weren't guilty. They'd done some pretty ghastly things in their young lives, but killing Constable Davis wasn't one of them. And I was able to persuade the jury of that.'

'Was it a tough fight?'

'As these things go, yes. The judge was dead set against the two kids—there was no doubt in his mind that they'd shot the policeman. But there was more to it than the facts any of us knew. As I told you, a lawyer is sheltered from his clients. He doesn't even bother to find out whether they're really innocent or not, usually. In this case, there were reasons why Morgan and Outram had been arrested. It was a confused gangland squabble, involving a prostitute called Mavis Walker. She had a bitter grudge against Billy Morgan and Butch Outram because they'd killed her fancy man. Or so she said. And she'd tried to set up her own version of justice.'

'Did she appear at the trial—this Mavis Walker?'

'She was the prosecution's chief witness,' he said, his golden eyes darkening. 'She was lying through her teeth, of course. But she was unshakeable. She claimed to have been at the bank that morning. And to have recognised the two accused. She had a mass of details, confirmation, evidence. She was all set to put Morgan and Outram away for the rest of their lives.'

'But you won the case, didn't you? One of your colleagues told me it was a brilliant defence.'

'Yeah. Brilliant.' His voice was harsh. 'It was a struggle, an uphill struggle all the way. But in the end I took Mavis Walker's evidence apart, piece by piece. That obstinate jury resisted me all the way, but in the end I won through. Even though I was already beginning to have doubts, to become uncertain.'

'Uncertain about what?'

'About Morgan and Outram. About what I was doing. About the people I mixed with. After all, these two kids had probably killed half a dozen men in their time, besides all the beatings and stabbings they'd dealt out. Why shouldn't they go to jail?'

'Because they weren't guilty of this particular charge,' Storm exclaimed, and he nodded.

'Yes. Because in this case they were innocent. That's why I got them off. It was a minor triumph.' He moved another piece. 'Checkmate.'

'Something else happened, didn't it?' she asked. 'What?'

'As I walked out of the court-room after the acquittal,' he said, his voice quiet and slow, 'I saw Mavis Walker. Her face was like a ghost's—dreadful. I don't think I've ever seen such fear in human eyes before. She knew she was doomed. My success had meant her destruction. And the kids' acquittal had meant her death sentence.'

Storm stared at him in horror. 'Did they—?'

'They ripped her apart,' he said quietly. 'They found her in a Soho club, dragged her into the lavatory, and killed her there.'

'Oh no . . .'

'Oh, yes. Because I'd been so bloody clever in getting those two thugs off, Mavis Walker was dead. Hacked to bits in a sordid little lavatory in Soho.'

'Jason,' she whispered. 'It wasn't your fault—'

'Wasn't it? But for me, it wouldn't have happened. And this time Morgan and Outram took care to have a cast-iron alibi. Billy Morgan even phoned me, can you believe that? *Justice is done, Mr Bentley*, he told me. *Justice is done.*' Jason swept the pieces into the box and stood up, his face set and bitter. 'I haven't slept since then. And I still don't know whether I'm ever going back to the Bar again.'

Storm watched him in horror, thinking of her stupid, cruel words to him this morning. God! Could anything have been worse-timed? She was lucky he hadn't killed her! Her own words came back to her, bitter, vicious words that must have poured acid into the raw wound. No wonder he despised her, looked at her with hate in his eyes. She rose, her heart thudding, and reached out a hand.

'For God's sake, don't blame yourself,' she said

urgently. 'There was nothing you could have done to prevent it, it wasn't even your quarrel—'

'I don't need your advice,' Jason interrupted brusquely. 'What you said this morning was right. I got those two murderers off—to kill again.'

'But—but—you couldn't have let them go to jail for a crime they didn't commit, Jason!'

'Don't you think I haven't argued the thing in my head one way and the other a thousand times?' He thrust his hands into his pockets and stared into the dying fire with bitter eyes. 'That's why I've chosen this race. It's my own form of therapy. To enable me to think the whole sordid business through, and come to some kind of a decision about my life.'

'Your life?'

'My career, to put it bluntly.'

Storm looked at him with deep concern, not liking the lines of strain that were now visible around that passionate mouth.

'You're a brilliant lawyer, Jason,' she said gently. 'You've got a spectacular career ahead of you—'

'I've got my *life* ahead of me,' he snarled. 'My career comes second to that, Storm!'

'But you've got a gift for law,' she reminded him quietly. 'It's something very special, Jason—something you can't simply abandon. It could mean hope for hundreds, even thousands of people—'

'That wasn't what you were saying this morning,' he retorted, meeting her eyes with cold anger.

Storm nodded, the firelight glinting in her hair.

'You're right. But maybe I've grown up a little between this morning and this evening, Jason. And I've been wondering what it would mean to be accused of a

crime you didn't commit—to be unable to defend yourself—to have no one to speak for you.' She shuddered.
'It doesn't bear thinking of!'

'I see,' he rejoined with irony. 'And what about the
other aspect of it—the aspect you were so vocal about
this morning? What about the times I get guilty people
off to commit more crimes against a helpless society?'

'I can't believe that happens very often,' she
answered, looking up into his face with gentle green
eyes.

He stared down at her, then shook his head slowly.

'No, it doesn't happen often. But what's the difference between one death and a hundred? They're on your
conscience with equal weight, aren't they?'

'Maybe. But your father hanged people as a judge—
mightn't one of them have been innocent? Against all
the odds? The victim of a horrible coincidence?'

'What are you getting at?'

'I'm getting at the fact that we're only human. We
don't have divine insight into people's minds—and when
we administer the law, we have to accept that once in a
while—even if it's only one in a million—there'll be
mistakes. That doesn't mean we could live without law.'

Jason was watching her, his eyes dropping from her
eyes to her mouth. He shrugged. 'Maybe what you say is
true. It's the way I used to think—a long time ago.'

'Jason, I said a lot of damned silly things this morning.
But I know this—I'd rather you were a man who tried to
help people, no matter what they'd done, than a man
who wanted to punish them, no matter what they'd
done.'

Storm had put her hand on the warm skin of his arm as
she spoke, and now found herself close up to him,

staring into the most beautiful, most masculine eyes she had ever known. Tawny-green eyes with fierce flecks of gold in them, fringed with thick black lashes. He glanced down at her slim fingers on the thickness of his forearm and shook his head slightly.

'I may not admire your personality,' he said, his voice husky in a way that robbed her of her breath, 'but I'm not immune to your physical beauty, Storm. And right now I happen to need a woman very badly. So don't look at me like that.' A bitter smile tugged at his lips. 'Whatever else they may have done, Morgan and Outram have certainly wrecked my social life—and that includes my love-life.'

'Your father told me that the girl who was going to be your partner—' She hesitated, not sure how to continue.

'Her name was Helena Salisbury,' he said drily. 'Yes—she walked out on me, just like the rest of them. I'd thought that she was different, that she would understand, but—' He shrugged expressively.

'Couldn't you go to her? I mean, explain things—try and make it up?'

'What for?' he asked acidly. 'Helena showed me exactly what she was like when she left me. Besides,' he said, staring at Storm, 'I'm not in the mood for romantic stupidities right now. I simply couldn't handle any emotional entanglements.' He reached out and touched her lips with his finger, stroking the satiny skin. 'On the other hand,' he growled, 'I'm very much in need of physical reassurance. I'm sure you know what I mean.'

She turned away, her heart racing, with the memory of that wonderful face indelibly burned on her mind.

'I'm sorry,' she said, her own voice uncertain. 'I simply wanted to make a point—that you shouldn't let this horrible business weigh on your mind. You don't deserve the guilt—it wasn't your fault.'

'I wish I could persuade myself as cleverly as you have,' he commented. 'You should try the law yourself, Virtuous Lady.'

'Maybe I will,' she said lightly, then ventured to look at him again. 'Have you—' She stopped, then went on timidly, 'have you really not slept since that trial?'

'Not properly. A few snatches off and on. Every time I drift off I see Mavis Walker's face—'

'Jason, don't!' she urged, putting out her hand to him again. The firelight had turned his eyes to pools of liquid gold; and there was an expression in them now that was making her knees weak. What had he meant when he had said he wasn't immune to her physical beauty? Did he really find her attractive? The thought made her senses swim.

'Your skin is like velvet, Storm. Did you know that?'

She stared at him, hypnotised. Jason reached out a hand and brushed her hair with the backs of his fingers, a delicate caress that made her shudder inside. 'And your hair,' he said quietly. 'It's so very beautiful.' He twisted a golden strand of it around a finger, his eyes intent on it. 'It's thick and heavy—as though it was actually made of spun gold.'

'I inherited it from my mother,' she said with a catch in her voice. What was he doing to her? Did he know that his touch had made her weak inside, made her heart shake?

'Tell me about your parents,' he commanded, sitting down before the fire again and patting the space next to him.

Storm sat down, grateful to be off her suddenly-melting legs, and told him—haltingly at first, then with a rush as the memories returned. About her father's uncertain career in politics—the tension of elections and defeats, the whirl of political life. About the deep love that was between him and her mother, her quiet, smiling mother who had been so loyal to her family. About the accident. And the loneliness bordering on despair. And the long lonely struggle since then.

'So you got your degree?'

'A very mediocre one. English Lit., and Italian. It's never been of the slightest use to me.'

'It will be,' he said cryptically. 'Maybe it's been you who've been wrong—not your degree.'

'Maybe,' she said in a small voice. Jason was leaning on one arm, his face close to hers, his eyes idly watching her lips as she talked. The expression on his face was beginning to give her butterflies again. The fire had died down to a sea of embers again, a glowing ruby patch that filled the room with an infinitely warm, infinitely peaceful light. Jason reached out and trailed one finger down Storm's cheek, raising gooseflesh all over her body.

'I suppose men have been chasing you since you were sixteen?' he asked, brushing her cheek with his knuckles.

'I've never had much time for men,' she said nervously, aware that she was in grave danger of rubbing her cheek against his hand like an adoring cat!

'I almost believe you,' he said with gentle mockery. 'Your eyes can get very cool indeed, Virtuous Lady. But do girls get to the age of twenty-two these days without at least twenty-two boy-friends behind them?'

'I told you,' she said, her breath becoming ragged

under the influence of Jason's touch, 'I've never had time for men.'

'Maybe there's time now,' he suggested in a gentle growl, leaning forward.

CHAPTER FIVE

His lips were warm and firm against hers, his fingers still brushing her cheek. Storm drew back, her pulses racing.

'Jason, don't be silly,' she said unevenly.

'Your lips are like velvet, too,' he said, his eyes deep and intoxicating on hers. She knew he was going to kiss her again, but could not move to stop him. The fire hissed quietly beside them, its warm crackles and whispers the only sound disturbing the peace in the quiet room. She had expected his kiss to be aggressive, abrasive—like his mood had been throughout the day. Instead, it was gentle and insistent. His lips were warm, pressing against hers, exploring her mouth in a way that was beginning to make her head swim. Again she tried to draw back, but strong arms slid round her shoulders, lowering her on to her back. She stared up dizzily into Jason's splendid face, her breath coming fast and light.

'I don't think this is very sensible,' she said nervously.

'Why not?' he asked, brushing the hollow of her throat with his lips.

Storm tried to fight back the moan that rose in her throat.

'Because we agreed to keep personal feelings out of this—'

'I am,' he murmured. 'Aren't you?' He leaned over her, kissing the side of her neck, caressing the warm skin under her hair with his mouth.

'But—' she gasped.

'There aren't any buts. We don't have to like each other to do this, do we? And I did warn you, Storm—this is all I can handle right now—just this, with no emotional baggage attached.' His kisses were so light and gentle that they were making her mind swim. His lips drew a line of fire across the underneath of her chin. She could smell his hair, the warm tang of his skin. Beginning to feel desperate, she pushed at his shoulder, turning her head away. The broad muscles of his chest stirred under her palm, suggesting the controlled power in that hard, supremely beautiful body. *And right now I happen to need a woman very badly*. His breath was warm against her cheek as he took her earlobe between his teeth and tugged gently.

'Please, no!' She writhed away from him, feeling her back growing damp with perspiration.

'Why not? It's something we both need.'

'You're wrong,' she panted. 'I don't need this, Jason—'

'Don't you?' He ran fingers that were suddenly rough through her hair, making her gasp. 'I think you do, Storm. Why try and deny it?'

She clenched her mouth shut as he bent to kiss her again, closing her eyes. She was determined not to respond to him. Damn him! He was so expert, so authoritative. No doubt he had seduced dozens of women right here in front of this crackling, aromatic fire!

His tongue ran lightly across the line of her mouth, trailing intoxicating fire from corner to corner. Against her will, she could feel every muscle in her body relaxing, her arms beginning to slide around his neck, one hand finding the crisp warmth of his thick hair.

Her lips were parting under the passionate, gentle insistence of his. He could have forced her mouth open, she knew that—but he had chosen to make her surrender voluntarily to him. Blindly, she tried to resist him, tried to keep her teeth clenched, but they parted against her will. Suddenly it was as though some unbelievably wonderful firework had exploded in her mind, showering brilliance and colour through the darkness. She found her back arching upwards, thrusting her breasts against his hard chest. Her fingers clenched in his hair—and then she was lost in a kiss more utterly sensual, more bone-melting, than anything she had ever dreamed of. His body was fierce and hard against hers, their mouths locked together in a sweetness that was scalding, enveloping her like fire . . .

'Jason,' she gasped as he drew back to smile down at her. 'Don't do this to me! Let me up.'

'Stop playing the innocent,' he purred. 'Your kisses tell me everything I want to know, Storm Calderwood. Why make an issue out of it?'

'Because it *is* an issue,' she said, sitting up weakly, aware of trembling stomach-muscles. 'I'm not the sort of woman who jumps into bed with every second man!'

'Who said anything about bed? Isn't this comfortable enough?' he mocked.

'You don't even like me!' she protested sharply.

Jason shrugged. 'So? That's got nothing to do with this. This is something our bodies need. I don't have to like you to make love to you, do I?'

'How can you even talk like that?' she gasped. 'I've never met anyone as callous as you—never!'

'I'm just being practical, Storm.' He reached out, unhooking the buttons on the front of her blouse. Her head dropped, her heavy, golden hair brushing his fingers helplessly.

'Jason, don't do this, for God's sake—'

'I'm doing it for my own sake,' he said, his voice deep and rough with desire. He slipped the thin material of her blouse aside, and trailed his fingers across the full, smooth swell of her breast. She gasped, feeling her whole body shudder and change, and leaned forward against him, her forehead resting against his. A profound ache had started inside her. In the silence, his fingers brushed the ultra-sensitive skin gently, maddeningly slowly. Storm was aware of her mind slipping into the fiery depths of desire. His hand on her breasts was an agony, an ecstasy, a sweet torment that had to be brought to some conclusion, had to be stopped—

When at last he cupped her breast in his hand, her nipple thrusting into his palm, Storm moaned out loud, shaking her head, and pulling back. Any further than this, she knew, and she would no longer have any control over what happened to her—she would be Jason's, utterly and completely. She pulled her blouse closed with trembling fingers, whispering, 'No—not like this.'

'How, then? Must you be wooed and flattered, like other stupid women? I thought you were more sensible than that, Virtuous Lady,' he mocked.

'It's got nothing to do with sense,' she retorted, shaking her hair out of her eyes. 'This isn't right, Jason— it's not what I want.'

'You're not trying to tell me you've never had a man, are you?' In one lithe movement he had pulled his T-shirt off, and the glow of the embers was soft on the sheen of his skin. He was magnificently-built, each muscle distinct under his silky skin, broad-shouldered but not heavy. Storm tried to tear her eyes away from him, but he was too beautiful. He pulled her to him again, and the touch of his hot, naked body was more than she could bear. She clung to him with confused passion, offering her face to his kisses—passionate, dizzying kisses that came like scalding rain on her eyelids, her cheeks, her temples, her mouth . . .

As his hands slipped under her blouse to claim her shuddering skin, her own fingers dug into the firm muscles of his back, and she met his kiss with a blazing passion that had them both gasping and dizzy.

'God,' he whispered fiercely, 'I need you so much, Storm! You're so beautiful—'

'It's not me you need,' she wailed, burying her face in the musky skin of his neck. 'You just need any woman, any female body to give you comfort, make you sleep!'

'Then give me that comfort,' he commanded, his lion's eyes hungry, demanding.

'I can't,' she said with a little sob. 'I can't, Jason. Not like this! Not so crudely, without love—'

'Why not, for heaven's sake? Are you a virgin?'

'You know I am,' she said, drawing back, and fastening the buttons on her blouse with hands that shook like autumn leaves.

'As a matter of fact, I didn't know,' he said gently, stroking her hair. 'But is that such a terrible thing?'

'It's got nothing to do with it,' she answered, aching for him with a sweet pain that was like nothing she had ever known. 'It's not the fact that I'm a virgin that matters—it's just what we're doing, the way we're doing it—how can I let you use my body, when you don't even care a damn for me?'

'I'm prepared to let you use *my* body on those terms,' he said quietly.

'It's not enough!'

'I see,' he sneered, 'you need lies, boxes of chocolates, bunches of tawdry flowers—'

'A little affection, a little genuine feeling would do,' she retorted. They both stood up, anger growing in their eyes again.

'God! So you've been playing around with me all this while?' Jason demanded furiously.

'You started,' she snapped, bitterly angry and hurt.

'I'm beginning to understand what kind of a woman you are,' he said with acid sarcasm. 'The kind of woman who likes to tease—'

'No!'

'—the kind of woman who'll lead a man on until she's got what she wanted, and then—'

'Jason, stop!' she cried angrily. 'How can you talk like this?'

'How can you behave like this?' he demanded, his face a mask of anger.

Storm turned away, unwilling to show him the bright tears in her green eyes.

'Because it's the way I'm made,' she retorted. 'And I can't help that.'

There was a tense silence.

'Then tell me one thing—truthfully—have you felt nothing at all tonight?'

'That's a question I don't want to think about—'

'Answer it, damn it all. Look at me! Don't you want me? Desire me?'

She looked at him with brimming, angry eyes that glistened like wet emeralds in the soft light.

'You know I do,' she whispered. 'Damn you for it!'
She turned blindly, and ran up to her room, sobbing.

The next day was unhappy and strained. Storm and
Jason seemed to be at loggerheads, the events of the
night before hanging over them like a cloud. His replies
to her remarks were monosyllabic, his eyes cold and
hard. Lockwood Bentley, after trying in vain to inject a
little warmth into the atmosphere, eventually gave up,
and took Storm on a tour of his little farm. His evident
pride in the place, and its considerable beauty, both
cheered Storm slightly. Last night's experience has
shaken her profoundly, forced her to reconsider a lot of
things about herself. The ease with which Jason had
collapsed her defences was sobering. Sobering, too, was
the thought that she had been impulsive and stupid in
her initial assessment of his legal work. It depressed her
to think that she was capable of such mistaken judgments—she who had always prided herself on her ability
to get to the root of things.

She accompanied the Judge, smiling and nodding to
his kindly talk, but thinking hard all the same. What had
hurt her more than anything had been Jason's calm
assumption that he could make love to her—that they
could share their bodies—without the slightest spark of
affection, let alone love. And he had almost swept her
into conceding. Even now, as she patted the glossy neck
of the Judge's thoroughbred admiringly, the memory of
Jason's touch, Jason's lips, sent a voluptuous inward
shudder through her. So this was Storm the cool and
untouchable, was it? She rebuked herself angrily. To
have succumbed to a stranger's touch like that! What

was she—a moony teenager? Never again, she swore to herself, would she let Jason Bentley upset her again. Never! The Judge, catching sight of her determined expression as she glared unseeingly at his prize boar, was quite startled.

When they got back to the farmhouse, Jason had drawn up a contract specifying the terms they had agreed to earlier that week. He handed it to her coldly, and after reading it through, she nodded.

'It seems all right,' she agreed. He passed her his gold Parker silently, and she uncapped the pen, hesitated—then signed her name at the bottom.

'Good,' he said shortly, passing her her own copy, and sitting down opposite her. 'Now,' he said drily, his eyes dispassionate, 'the race begins on the fifth of next month. That's barely a week away—and we've got a lot of preparations to make. Among them is getting you some suitable clothes. Especially something to wear during the race itself. How are you off for coats?'

'I've still got an old astrakhan that was my mother's,' she ventured.

Jason shook his head.

'You'll need something glamorous. And warm. Also scarves, hats, gloves—that sort of thing. There's also,' he added, his mouth tugging into an ironic grimace, 'the question of these silly dances before and after the race.' He looked at her speculatively—and again Storm was reminded of a racehorse owner surveying a prospective brood mare. 'I think we'd better go and see the vermouth people tomorrow morning. And in the afternoon we'd better try and get you some clothes. Agreed?'

'If you say so,' she said with ironic acquiescence.

He shot her a sharp glance.

'I don't like these trappings any more than you do, Storm. We just have to put up with them.'

'Of course,' she said coolly. 'Just as you have to put up with me in your balloon.'

His eyes were cold. 'Yes. It's a necessary evil.' He glanced at his watch, then stood up with the quick, lithe movements that were typical of him. She recalled, in a flash, that splendid torso in the firelight, and bit the thought angrily back. 'I'm going to take you back to London now,' he informed her. 'You'd best get ready.'

'Nothing,' she told him drily, 'would give me greater pleasure!'

The pokeyness of her own flat depressed her after the spacious glamour of the Bentley estate. Jason had dropped her at her front door, and she had been unable to fight back a pang of loss as he had driven off. Sunday evening, dreary and lonely, extended ahead of her. Kelly and Paul had gone to Devon for the weekend— and there was nobody else in London she cared to see. Unwilling to cook, she went out for fish and chips, and dropped most of it in the rubbish bin as uneatable. Sunday evening fare on television was as unpalatable as the soggy chips, and she curled up in the sofa with a paperback, losing herself in the vicarious enjoyment of someone else's adventures.

With the perversity of human nature, she had just begun to enjoy her book when the doorbell rang, and muttered resentfully as she went to answer it. It was Steve Manning, smiling rather ruefully.

'I've just had a hell of a row with Les,' he informed her. He and his girl-friend had recently got together again. 'She's gone storming off to her sister's. So I've come to you for comfort.'

'Come on in,' she grinned. 'Coffee? Or something stronger?'

'No, thank you,' he said with a shudder. 'The row started over my being out at the pub all last night with some old friends.'

She made him tea, feeling sorry for him. Steve and Lesley, she knew, were deeply in love with each other, a bright, happy couple whom it was a pleasure to know. Now and then Steve's occasional reversion to the wicked days of his youth provoked a row—soon patched up, but amusingly ferocious while it lasted.

Storm listened to his tale of woe, trying not to smile, and assured him that Lesley would be back soon enough. He began to look somewhat comforted.

'What about you?' he asked. 'Did you let Kelly and Paul talk you out of your balloon race?'

'No,' she smiled. 'As a matter of fact, I signed the contract this morning.' She explained the bare bones of her agreement with Jason Bentley, and he listened, a wise glint in his bright blue eyes.

'It all sounds very exciting,' he commented. 'But you don't look particularly happy, Storm.' The lift at the end turned the sentence into a question, and she bit her lip.

'Well, if you want to know, ı find Jason Bentley a rather disturbing man.'

'In what way?'

'He's—well, it's hard to say what he is. Very clever, very masculine, very hard and ruthless. And he doesn't like me one little bit.'

Steve raised his eyebrows, holding out his cup for more coffee.

Harlequin Presents...

VIOLET WINSPEAR

time of the temptress

Harlequin Presents...

SALLY WENTWORTH

say hello to yesterday

GET 4 BOOKS FREE

Harlequin Presents...

CHARLOTTE LAMB

man's world

Harlequin Presents...

ANNE MATHER

born out of love

Say Hello to Yesterday

Holly Weston had done it all alone.

She had raised her small son and worked her way up to features writer for a major newspaper. Still the bitterness of the the past seven years lingered.

She had been very young when she married Nick Falconer—but old enough to lose her heart completely when he left. Despite her success in her new life, her old one haunted her.

But it was over and done with—until an assignment in Greece brought her face to face with Nick, and all she was trying to forget. . . .

Time of the Temptress

The game must be played his way!

Rebellion against a cushioned, controlled life had landed Eve Tarrant in Africa. Now only the tough mercenary Wade O'Mara stood between her and possible death in the wild, revolution-torn jungle.

But the real danger was Wade himself—he had made Eve aware of herself as a woman.

"I saved your neck, so you feel you owe me something," Wade said. "But you don't owe me a thing, Eve. Get away from me." She knew she could make him lose his head if she tried. But that wouldn't solve anything. . . .

Your Romantic Adventure Starts Here.

Born Out of Love

It had to be coincidence!

Charlotte stared at the man through a mist of confusion. It was Logan. An older Logan, of course, but unmistakably the man who had ravaged her emotions and then abandoned her all those years ago.

She ought to feel angry. She ought to feel resentful and cheated. Instead, she was apprehensive—terrified at the complications he could create.

"We are not through, Charlotte," he told her flatly. "I sometimes think we haven't even begun."

Man's World

Kate was finished with love for good.

Kate's new boss, features editor Eliot Holman, might have devastating charms—but Kate couldn't care less, even if it was obvious that he was interested in her.

Everyone, including Eliot, thought Kate was grieving over the loss of her husband, Toby. She kept it a carefully guarded secret just how cruelly Toby had treated her and how terrified she was of trusting men again.

But Eliot refused to leave her alone, which only served to infuriate her. He was no different from any other man. . . or was he?

These FOUR free Harlequin Presents novels allow you to enter the world of romance, love and desire. As a member of the Harlequin Home Subscription Plan, you can continue to experience all the moods of love. You'll be inspired by moments so real... so moving... you won't want them to end. So start your own Harlequin Presents adventure by returning the reply card below. <u>DO IT TODAY!</u>

'He doesn't? Then why is he taking you with him on this race?'

'Because he needs me,' she said with a bitter little smile. After a minute's hesitation, she told him about the race and the necessity to keep up a glamorous appearance.

'So—why doesn't he like you? Can't you charm him round with those emerald eyes of yours?'

'I'm afraid not. I was extremely rude to him—and I don't think he's ever going to forgive me for it.'

'There's something you haven't mentioned, Storm.' Steve's boyish smile was grave. 'How *you* feel about *him*. Does he attract you, by any chance?'

'Not in the slightest,' she retorted fiercely. So fiercely that Steve's eyebrows arched again. 'I hate that sort of man,' she went on hurriedly, 'that sort of aggressive man who thinks every woman is his for the taking. He's the most arrogant person I've ever known.'

'Indeed,' murmured Steve. 'I know I shouldn't be asking this, Storm—but you're an old friend, and I think I know you quite well—'

'Has he made a pass at me?' she volunteered, and he nodded. 'I don't know if you could even call it a pass,' she said wearily, closing her eyes. 'He simply wanted me to give in to him. No strings attached, no emotional ties.'

Steve looked at her sympathetically.

'Not everyone is as sentimental or as moral about sex as you are, Storm,' he said gently.

She opened her eyes.

'I'm not sentimental or moral!' she exclaimed.

'Oh yes, you are,' he said firmly. 'I know you like to make out that you're so cool and hard-headed, Storm— but you aren't. And it's about time you started realising

that. If you really were as cold and calculating as you like
to think, then you'd have jumped into bed with Jason
Bentley straight away—if you'll allow me to speak
directly.' Storm stared at him with wide green eyes,
nonplussed.

He went on, 'You're very vulnerable, Storm. All the
more so because you happen to be a very beautiful
woman who will always be attractive to men. As for
Jason Bentley—well, I reckon you don't know very
much about him. And despite your protestations, it
sounds to me very much as though you like him. A lot.'

She looked down at her hands, feeling her cheeks
grown suddenly hot.

'Watch yourself, Storm,' Steve warned her. 'Men can
be totally ruthless when it comes to women. Then again,
they can be angels. A lot depends on how well you know
each other—and how sensibly you behave.' He swal-
lowed the last of his coffee and smiled at her. 'Don't get
too caught up in hating Jason Bentley. Or the other way
around. Okay—lecture over!'

The publicity officer for the vermouth firm was delighted
with Storm. A portly, handsome man, he had fussed
over her with the delight of a collie-fancier being shown
a particularly fine specimen. She thought he would have
liked to examine her teeth, but that good breeding
prevented him. But he agreed that Storm would add
considerably to the advertising appeal of the balloon
flight.

'There's as big a potential in this,' he assured them
earnestly, 'as there is in Formula One racing.' When he
and Jason had come down to talking money, the figures
under discussion startled Storm; she hadn't realised

before quite how expensive it was to mount an operation of this sort. Somewhat dazed by this talk of hundreds and thousands, she had accompanied Jason out of the building and to a nearby restaurant, where they had eaten a light salad lunch. Afterwards, Jason glanced at her.

'Thank you for looking good, by the way,' he said drily. 'You helped a lot.'

Storm had taken care of her appearance, wearing her best outfit, a cream silk dress with a matching jacket, and the heavy rope of pearls that her father had bought her mother. She looked good, yes—but she was slowly becoming irritated with the sense that she was merely an animated tailor's dummy, an attractive prop to embellish male achievement. She had never got into the habit of thinking about her appearance in great detail. Until very recently, she had not considered the fact that she was beautiful, accepting her figure and looks with gratitude because both were so healthy, but not with vanity. It was a new experience to discover that she was actually beautiful, someone who could be chosen to advertise vermouth in those glamorous ads on television.

And the publicity agent, his teeth glinting in his wide smile, had hinted strongly that there might be a lot more work for her, depending on how the balloon race was received. 'You've got the *carriage*,' he assured her, 'you've got the *style*.' That, too, had irritated her. Was it quite polite, she wondered, for a strange man to make personal comments about her looks and figure? Women's liberation had never exerted any interest for Storm, but she was beginning to chafe under the suggestion that she was simply a beautiful object. So when Jason thanked her for looking good, she merely gave him a cold little smile and asked for more coffee.

In his immaculate grey suit, she reflected, he was like the answer to a maiden's prayer, a real deb's delight. Until you looked a little closer, and saw a man who would eat maidens for breakfast, a powerful, hard man, whose splendid hazel eyes held the authoritative light of a lion's. He glanced at his watch.

'Shall we go?'

The interior of the Lamborghini was warm from the sun, and smelled deliciously of leather and expensive aftershave. Storm sat, lost in thought, while Jason made some notes in his pocketbook. Then he looked up.

'Let's get you a coat, shall we? Is there any particular place you want to go to?'

'I don't know,' she answered. 'Er—Marks and Spencer's?'

'I don't think so,' he smiled. 'There's a place in Regent Street that might have what we want.' He turned the key in the ignition.

Rossignol's in Regent Street was quite literally *the* most expensive shop Storm had ever set foot in. There were no price tags on the six stunning coats in the window, one of them a glistening cascade of ebony sable that would, Storm knew, cost as much as a big house. And inside Rossignol's was a world of leather and suede and fur, of plush, velvety fabrics and dramatically-styled jackets, of sable and fox and mink. These were the clothes that only the very rich wore, the exquisite coats and furs and hats that you saw on the covers of *Paris-Match* or *Stern*, casually draped over the shoulders or arms of famous women.

Determined not to be overawed, she turned to Jason with a cool smile.

'Do you do a lot of your shopping here? Your women must be very pampered.'

'I'm not in the habit of pampering "my women", as you call them,' he told her drily. 'This is an investment, Storm.'

'You flatter me,' she said with a touch of bitterness. 'I only hope I come up to expectations.'

'You're doing all right,' he said shortly, and his arrogance made her grit her teeth. The saleslady glided towards them with a businesslike glint in her eye; but as the manager caught sight of the tall, authoritative man and the beautiful blonde, he elbowed her discreetly back behind the counter, and oozed up with a smile.

'May I assist you, madame?'

Storm glanced at Jason. 'Yes, please,' she said. 'I'd like a coat.'

The manager's eyes flattered her figure.

'Of course,' he beamed, and bowed very low.

Storm was suddenly grateful for her choice of her best cream suit for the morning's shopping. They were not going to get out of Rossignol's under a couple of hundred pounds, that was certain. And if that was what Jason Bentley wanted, then—

'Oh, something warmer than that,' Jason was saying. 'What about that one on the rack?'

'That's chamois, sir,' said the manager with a gleam in his eye. 'It is a beautiful coat, is it not?' He slipped the unbelievably soft and pliable fawn coat over Storm's shoulders, and she turned in front of the mirror. It was superbly cut, with wide wing collars; and the leather itself was lovely, ranging from chocolate to pale gold, as soft as thick silk.

'It's beautiful,' she sighed. 'Chamois?' She examined

it dubiously. 'This isn't the stuff they make wash-leathers out of, is it?'

'Oh no, madam,' deprecated the manager with a smile at Jason. 'This is the skin of a Spanish antelope, madam. I might tell you that the American President's wife—'

'I don't want it,' said Storm, slipping the beautiful thing off.

Jason raised an eyebrow. 'Why not?'

'I don't want anything that's been made out of slaught-ered wild-life,' she said. 'I don't think women should adorn themselves with the skins of beautiful animals.'

The manager glanced at Jason, then laughed politely.

'Oh, but madam,' he said, stroking the beautiful leather with a superior smile, 'there's no need to be over-sentimental. These creatures are—'

'She doesn't want it,' said Jason, and the edge of steel beneath the velvet of his voice wiped the smile off the manager's lips.

'Of course,' he said hurriedly. 'I was merely—'

'What about something in wool?' asked Jason, getting up to examine a rack of coats near him. He hooked one off the rail and held it out. 'Do you like this?'

Storm took it, rubbing her fingers over the immediate warmth of the wool. It was a long, pure white coat with a high collar at the back and deep pockets, as light and as warm as sunlight. She slipped it on, the manager assist-ing from behind, and surveyed the result in a mirror. The long white sweep of the coat flattered her figure, the purity of its colour setting off the gold in her skin to perfection.

'It's pretty,' she acknowledged.

'And the animal gave it up willingly,' said Jason with

dry irony. He stepped behind her to examine the hang of the garment with a critical eye.

'Turn around,' he commanded. Storm pirouetted obligingly, feeling absurdly like a model in some private fashion show, and met his eyes. He was looking at her with such direct admiration that her heart lurched. She looked down, flushing. For all Jason was concerned, she knew, she might as well be absolutely naked! Her face as hot as though she really were standing before him without a stitch on, she turned away, and glanced at the coat again.

'I'm not sure if it's going to be warm enough,' she said.

'Oh, madam,' cooed the manager, scenting a sale, 'this is one of the warmest materials in the shop. And if I may say so,' he added, with a nervous glance at Jason, 'it looks very beautiful on you.'

She looked at Jason enquiringly. He shrugged slightly.

'It's up to you, Storm. Do you like it?'

'It's lovely,' she smiled, pressing the exquisitely soft fabric to her cheek. The pearl buttons lent the garment a shimmering beauty that delighted her. 'How much is it?' she asked the manager. Without blinking, he named a sum that was approximately twice Storm's monthly salary as the Sheik's governess. Jason, however, seemed unmoved.

'It's very glamorous,' he assured her. 'Have it, then, if you want it. And we'd better get some scarves while we're here.'

'Certainly, sir,' beamed the manager.

'And some gloves. And a hat.'

'That will be a positive pleasure, sir,' said the

manager, and Storm felt sure that every tooth in his head
was on show in that smile.

'It's wonderful what money can do, isn't it?' she
remarked to Jason as the manager scurried off. Her
smile was cool and bitterly ironic.

'Yes,' he said cruelly, 'I was forgetting what a moral
little creature you were.'

Hating him, she pulled off the white wool coat, and
the saleslady materialised behind her to take it, fluttering her bright blue eyelids in Jason's direction.

'Isn't it a lovely day, sir?' she mewed with a simper,
then caught sight of Storm's expression.

'I'll just go and wrap this up,' she gulped, her smile
vanishing.

The back seat of the Lamborghini was little more than
an extra cubbyhole (selfish car, thought Storm, selfish
man); and it was overflowing with expensive-looking
parcels by the time Jason pulled up outside Storm's flat
in Wright Street. Conversation had been minimal and
icy all the way back from Rossignol's, and in silence,
Storm prepared to gather her new possessions. Jason
uttered an exclamation of annoyance.

'Damn! I've forgotten I was supposed to meet one of
my clients tonight. I'll have to put him off.' He turned to
Storm, who was watching him over an arm-full of parcels. 'Would you let me come up to your flat and make a
phone call?'

'If you must,' she said inhospitably, not much re-
lishing the idea of Jason coming into her little flat. She
led him resentfully up to her flat, shouldered the door
open (she wouldn't allow him to carry any of the afternoon's purchases for her) and gestured disdainfully
towards the telephone.

'There it is—help yourself.'

She heaped the parcels willy-nilly on to the sofa. How delighted she would have been, in any other circumstances, with such a bonanza of beautiful new clothes! And how thrilled she would have been to have entertained any other man as handsome as Jason Bentley in her flat. She glanced at him surreptitiously as he barked his orders down the telephone. What a waste of a beautiful body, she thought bitterly. A man with such potent powers of physical attraction didn't have the right to be such a cold-blooded devil. She took in the tawny, fierce eyes, the curve of the passionate, mouth, the poised yet somehow tense stance of the athletic body. How would he look in court? she wondered. Distinctly formidable, she decided. The black silk gown, designed to add presence and dignity to ordinary men, on him would look magnificent, even majestic. As a cross-examiner, he would be intimidating. Very. Conscious of her covert stare, he looked up suddenly, meeting her eyes with that electric jolt which always shook her. She pointed to the kettle enquiringly, and he nodded curtly. Damn! She didn't want to have to entertain him. She wanted him to get out and go home as swiftly as possible. Yet she was obscurely pleased as she made him coffee. It was funny; but there was a special, uniquely feminine pleasure in making something—even if it was only a cup of coffee—for the man you loved.

She screwed the top on to the percolator and put it on the stove, then busied herself with her best cups and saucers. Would he like chocolate biscuits, she wondered, or should she—

The man you loved? A teacup slid through her nerveless fingers as she whipped round to stare through the kitchenette door at Jason, who was listening intently to what the other person was saying. Her heart was thudding painfully against her ribs, and she was abruptly aware that she was going to have to sit down.

She—Storm the cool, Storm the dispassionate—in love? In love with Jason Bentley? With the rudest, most arrogant man she had ever met? It was impossible! The abandoned cup rolled in a slow semi-circle across the melamine worktop, and Storm was just quick enough to catch it as it fell. What aberration, what fit of craziness had possessed her to think that she was in love with him? Dear God, what a preposterous idea! Quiet, she told her joyfully pounding heart, *be quiet, damn you!* It's not true! There's been some grotesque mistake—

'What's the hell's the matter?' Jason was standing in the doorway, watching her with cold eyes. 'Are you feeling ill?'

She gaped at him. It was the most extraordinary thing, but she had never noticed before what a stunning contrast those tawny-green eyes made to the black lashes, the black brows, the thick dark hair. It really was the secret of his fantastic looks. And the mouth, of course, that deliciously sensual mouth that could terrify and caress in the same moment. And the nose, naturally, that straight nose with the fine, flared nostrils—

'Storm!' He shook her, his eyes narrowing with worry. 'What's up, girl? Are you all right?'

'Oh,' she murmured, coming out of her reverie with a jolt, 'yes—er—I'm fine. I just—just had a sudden thought, that's all.'

'Well, thank God for that,' he said drily, his eyes still concerned. 'For a minute I thought you'd electrocuted yourself on the kettle.' She was staring at him with wide green eyes, as though seeing him for the very first time. Was it possible—that this was the man she was destined to love? Never! Love didn't simply arrive unannounced in the kitchen, over preparations for coffee. Love came by moonlight, with bunches of roses. And you didn't love people like Jason Bentley—you loved quite different people, like—like—Storm tried to conjure other male images out of her imagination. But there were none. There was no one. No one except this unbelievably powerful man—

'*Storm!*' Jason took her shoulders and shook her. 'What the hell is going on in your head? Do you want to lie down?'

'No,' she said, suddenly snapping back to normality with an effort, 'no—I'm fine. Go and sit down—I'll bring your coffee through in a minute.'

Her mind was racing as she made the coffee, trying to assimilate the discovery she had just made. *Might* have just made, she cautioned herself. Her fingers were unsteady, her heart still pounding. Dear heaven, she would have to be on her guard from now on—on guard every minute, every second. Because if Jason once suspected how deeply she was stirred by him, she would have no more defences against him. None at all.

She brought the tray through, to find him writing busily on his pad. At all costs she must appear natural.

'What's all this about a client?' she asked lightly, pouring the scalding, fragrant brew. 'I thought you'd abandoned law for a while?'

'Thanks,' he said absently, taking the cup from her. 'This is a case that's been coming up for a long time. I couldn't simply cancel it.'

'What's the charge?' she asked, watching the strong brown hands as he made quick, shorthand notes on his pad.

He looked up briefly. 'Hmm? Oh—nothing very glamorous. Embezzlement.'

'Oh,' she said. 'Is he guilty?'

He looked up irritably again. 'What?'

'Is he guilty?' she asked again.

Jason stared at her without seeing her, tawny eyes absent.

'Yes,' he said slowly. 'He's guilty all right. But there are mitigating circumstances—the poor old chap only borrowed the money to cover some urgent expenses. He'd intended to put it back. He was just caught too soon.' He was busy writing again. Storm stared resentfully at the intent face. Nothing in this life seemed to turn out as you expected it to, she thought wryly. Here she was, palpitating with what might be the most momentous discovery of her young life, sitting with aching heart and wet palms—and the only man she had ever felt a spark of feeling for in her life was sitting writing, ignoring her completely.

Without looking up, Jason suddenly said, 'Why don't you try that coat on again?'

'Okay,' she said happily, and jumped up to unwrap it from its glossy parcel.

'It's a pity it doesn't show your legs more,' he said absently. 'Advertisers love legs.'

'Do they?' she said in a chilly voice, shaking the fluffy white garment out.

'Mmm,' he said, looking up for a moment. 'So do the judges—remember that in Italy.'

'I'll do my best,' Storm said coldly as he bent to his

work again. She began unfastening the pearl buttons slowly, her happiness abruptly subdued.

'Come on,' snapped Jason without looking up. 'I haven't got much time.'

'I'm doing my best,' she gritted.

'Yeah—well, I want to make sure I haven't wasted my money.'

The white coat thumped into his chest with furious force. He looked up at her, astonished. 'What the—'

'I'm a human being, damn it,' she blazed at him.

Jason disentangled himself from the coat, his eyes wide with surprise.

'Of course you are—'

'Then treat me like one!'

He took in her white, furious face and glittering eyes.

'What's up with you, anyway?' he demanded. 'Haven't you just been given a beautiful wool coat—'

'Given?' she sneered. 'Not likely! It's been draped over me, with about as much sensitivity as though I were a tailor's dummy in some shop window!'

'Storm—'

'Well, I've had enough,' she told him bitterly. 'If you can't treat me like a human being—like a woman—then you can go on your damned race alone!'

He stared at her with cold eyes.

'I tried to treat you like a woman two nights ago—remember? But you didn't want that, either.'

'Is that the limit of your behaviour?' she demanded. 'You're either trying to use my body—whether I like it or not—or you're treating me as though I were some uncomplicated piece of business equipment!'

'This *is* a business arrangement,' he reminded her

icily. 'I thought we'd agreed that? I thought you were so cool and professional?'

'Being professional about things doesn't mean putting up with intolerable rudeness and insensitivity,' she retorted hotly. 'Just the opposite, in fact!'

'I'm not following you, Storm,' he said, his voice matching the glaciers in his eyes. He thrust the white coat aside and stood up, an unexpectedly formidable figure. 'I've never been enamoured of your style, young lady—but I thought you were at least above these hysterical female tantrums.'

'It's got nothing to do with being female,' she snapped. 'I don't understand you either, Jason. You seem to think you're the only person in the world who's got any troubles or worries—'

'On the contrary,' he said frigidly, 'I'm very much aware of other people's feelings. And what's more, I try and prevent my own worries from influencing the way I run my affairs—'

'You don't! You're the most callous, arrogant person I've ever met—'

'You're overwrought, Storm.' His face was angry now, his mouth compressed into that hard line she so dreaded. 'You'd better get some sleep. I don't know what the hell's got into you just now—'

'And you never will know, either,' she snapped, perilously close to tears, 'because you just don't give a damn—' Then she was in his arms, trying to fight back the sobs. What on earth was wrong with her? Somewhere above the emotional turmoil that was raging in her heart was a little cool portion of her mind that was watching with dismay. God, she hated him! She wanted to tear herself out of his arms and run, run a mile. Was this what love meant? This fury, this hurt anger, this irrational tempest in the heart?

He tilted her chin up roughly, and his mouth claimed hers, hard and fierce. With a sobbing moan, her mouth gave way to his, letting him thrust through the softness of her lips, plundering the sweetness within. Now desire was ruthless, pouring liquid flame into her body, her heart, her loins; her hands were finding their way beneath his shirt to claim the hard, sweet flesh of his shoulders. Jason crushed her to him, his body shuddering in a way that made her weak, and she moulded her body against the muscular outline of his strength, her hips thrusting forward, seeking his desire shamelessly. With a deep gasp, he dropped his hands to her hips, pulling her against him with intoxicating force as their mouths tussled, tasted, dissolved into a molten torment that was stronger, deeper than anything in the world.

Storm tore herself away from him, her breath ragged in her throat, and brushed her hair back with a shaking hand.

'No,' she whispered unevenly, 'don't make me lose my head . . .'

Jason stared at her with blazing eyes, his powerful chest panting; then he turned on his heel, his face set.

'I don't have the time to play these woman's games with you, Storm—I have to be in court by nine tomorrow. I'm leaving.' At the door, he turned to face her. 'Oh, and by the way—if you have any childish ideas about backing out of the race—don't. You signed a contract, remember?' His eyes were like ice. 'If you try and break it, I'll make you regret it, Storm. Very bitterly.' The door slammed hard.

Storm stared at it with brimming eyes, the memory of

his lips still burning on her mouth. Love? That discovery of hers wasn't going to make her life any easier. On the contrary, it was going to make it impossible. And within a week, they were going to be in Italy together!

CHAPTER SIX

'. . . in approximately twenty minutes. Local time is six-thirty p.m., and the temperature at Milan Airport is nineteen degrees. Thank you for flying with Alitalia. *Signore e signori, il capitano . . .*' Storm stared out of the window as the air hostess purred on. Italy was somewhere sixteen thousand feet beneath that sea of wispy cloud. Jason's eyes were shut. During the flight from Heathrow, they hadn't exchanged more than ten words. Which was nothing unusual; for the past week, relations between them had been strained. The days had rushed past in an ever-accelerating whirl of preparations and plans. There had been no time to think. And she was tired now, and somewhat tense. She glanced across at Jason's face. Underneath the tan, he too was looking tired. She wondered whether he had slept properly since the murder trial. She guessed not. She looked down at the strong hands lightly clasped in his lap. Elegant, powerful hands. Hands that had caressed her shuddering skin . . .

Storm shut her mind to the thought, and managed a smile for the air hostess as she surrendered her plastic cup. Milan was less than a quarter of an hour away. Then straight on to Cremona, where they were booked into the Imperial there ('No sense in going for second-best,' Jason had commented drily). And the day after tomorrow—the Trans-Alps Balloon Race, an extraordinary

113

farrago of glamour, sportsmanship, publicity, spectacle, danger.

How much danger? Jason had made her study the route of the race in detail. Cremona to Milan. Milan to Zurich. Zurich to Konstanz. Between Milan and Zurich, the map had been a mosaic of purple and white. Heights of over nine thousand feet—the Alps. And a long way to fall. Jason had made no attempt to minimise the dangers—over half of their journey would be over the Alps. But the early autumn, as he had pointed out, was usually a time of beautiful weather over the Alps. Nor was it unusual for balloons to rise to such heights. 'The main problems,' he had warned her, 'are cold and altitude. You can wrap up against the cold—but the altitude is more difficult. It'll make you lose concentration, for one thing; you'll find your head full of silly thoughts, and you might feel drowsy. At worst, it'll make you feel sick.'

'How sick?' Storm had asked apprehensively.

'Nothing that airsickness pills can't deal with,' he had said with a grim smile. 'It won't last long, either. There are just two big jumps to make—Oberwald and Grindelwald.'

The names had struck a slight chill into her heart, and she had stared at him apprehensively.

'You'll be able to console yourself,' Jason reminded her callously, 'with the view.'

With a squeal of tyres, the airliner touched down, and the massive reverse thrust of the engines tugged at them for a few seconds; then they were taxiing through the evening towards the air terminal.

The air was crisp and cool, and Jason sniffed at it, glancing at Storm. 'Snow,' he said shortly. 'Maybe tonight or tomorrow.'

Storm followed him through Customs and Immigration in the echoing modernity of Leonardo da Vinci Airport. The Avis car was waiting for them, a light blue Fiat, and Jason loaded their bags into the boot.

'I want to get straight on the road to Cremona,' he said. 'Agreed?'

'Agreed,' she said. 'I'm looking forward to some sleep—it's been a hectic week.'

He nodded a curt agreement. 'Are you hungry?'

'I could eat something,' she shrugged. Leaving her to sit in the car and stare at the never-ending stream of departing and arriving passengers, Jason disappeared, returning after five minutes with two fragrant pizzas and two big bottles of mineral water.

Storm tucked into the delicious snack with relish as he drove off. This was far from the stodgy, Cheddar-sprinkled item you got in England—it was a crisp, exotic, scented thing that made a hungry girl's senses swim.

'Only the Italians could devote such care and ingenuity to a take-away snack,' Jason commented, sucking his fingertips. They exchanged cautious smiles. And a little tingle of excitement—the first for days—prickled along Storm's spine. They were here—Italy! And the biggest adventure of her life was almost beginning. As if he sensed her mood and shared it, Jason's smile broadened into a grin that transformed his face.

'We made it,' he said quietly. And to Storm's amazement, he held out his left hand, palm up. After a second's hesitation, she took it in both her own and laid it on her lap, not daring to look at him, but suddenly happier than she had been for weeks.

Jason retrieved his hand after a few minutes to deal

with a succession of traffic lights and busy streets on
the outskirts of Milan—and then they were on the
broad, dark highway—the Autostrada del Sole—to
Cremona.

It was eight o'clock by the time they had reached
Cremona—and it was obvious at once that the city was
buzzing with the Balloon Race. The streets were
crowded, jammed with cars and happy pedestrians (only
Italians, Storm decided, of all the people in Europe,
really knew how to celebrate). The pavement cafés were
full, every lamp-post and tree bearing placards announc-
ing the big race.

As they slowed to a crawl to make their way through
the happy, busy streets to the Imperial, Storm noticed
that the balloon-sellers, universal sign of Italian holiday,
were doing a roaring trade. Every child—and not a few
adults—seemed to be holding bright balloons on strings,
most emblazoned with the logo of the race.

'What an atmosphere!' she commented. 'I didn't imagine that this race was so well publicised.'

'It's big business,' Jason assured her. A band was
playing in one of the public squares, and the joyful
strains of its music rose above the hooters and engines of
the traffic. Cremona was a lovely city, of long Renaiss-
ance façades and tree-lined boulevards. Storm stared
out of the Fiat's window at the happy faces in the cafés,
whole families, apparently, enjoying the delicious night
air and the delights of a glass of wine and a slice of pizza
or *torta*. Her spirits had lifted considerably, and they
both wound down their windows to share in the festivi-
ties a little. At a set of traffic lights, predictably fes-
tooned with balloons, they stopped. A crowd of young
girls flocked around them, laughing and calling to each

other. One, a devastatingly pretty creature of sixteen or seventeen, flashed a brilliant smile at Jason, and leaned through the window.

'*Ciao, bello,*' she giggled, and planted a sticky kiss full on his startled mouth.

The Imperial was a great sheet of tinted glass rising inappropriately out of the mediaeval roofs of the city, and they parked the car in a vast underground car-park beneath the hotel. Various uniformed flunkeys were instantly at hand to take care of car-keys, baggage, coats. But the sheen of sweat on the desk clerk's upper lip presaged trouble.

'I am desolated, *signore* and *signora*,' he moaned. 'But it is the stupidity of our booking clerk. And the confusion with the race—all these tourists,' he explained, waving at the crowded foyer, 'of course it should never have happened, but under the circumstances—'

'What are you trying to say?' asked Jason impatiently. 'We want to get to our rooms as soon as possible, please.'

'Alas, *signore*,' wailed the clerk, 'I am trying to explain—through the stupidity of the booking clerk—'

'You've missed our booking?' Jason demanded, his eyes freezing.

'No, no, no—not missed, *signore*.' He tried an ingratiating smile, 'Merely misunderstood. In the heat of the moment, with all these tourists—it's the balloon race, of course—'

'What arrangements *have* you made, then?' Storm asked.

'Alas, *signora*—' he spread apologetic hands out, 'not two single rooms, but one double room.'

'One double room?' They exchanged wary glances. 'Have you nothing else?' Jason asked irritably.

'I am desolated, *signore*—but no. It's this balloon race, you see—the whole town is jam-packed—'

'It'll have to do, then,' he said shortly. 'If that's all right with you, Storm?'

'I suppose it's all right,' she said. But the thought of spending a night in the same room as Jason Bentley had set butterflies fluttering in her stomach. Jason pulled his pen out and signed the register. Struck by a thought, he looked up into the pale, nervous face of the desk clerk.

'Are there two beds in this room, by the way?'

An unhappy expression crossed the man's face.

'The source of all the confusion, *signore*, was the similarity between your esteemed name and that of an American couple who—'

'How many beds are there in this room?' asked Jason icily.

The desk clerk gulped.

'*Signore*, it's the honeymoon suite.'

'The *honeymoon suite*?'

'The honeymoon suite, *signore*.' He tugged at his collar. 'Naturally,' he said with a feeble smile, 'we will only be charging the *signore* the rate for two single room—'

'Blast and damn!' Jason looked at Storm with angry eyes and set mouth. 'Haven't you got anything else?'

'It's the balloon race, *signore*,' explained the clerk miserably. 'The whole town is full—'

'What a damned mess!' Jason snarled.

'*Signore*,' said the clerk anxiously, 'this is probably the only free room in Cremona tonight. I strongly advise you to take it!'

Jason stared at Storm again, his expression suggesting that she might be the carrier of any number of deadly contagious diseases.

'I don't snore,' she assured him with a slight smile.

His eyes were sardonic. He sighed. 'I suppose this situation has its funny aspects,' he said drily. 'But I'm damned if I can see them.'

They remained silent as the lift whooshed them up to the eminence of the eighteenth storey. And they were silent as the porter bustled ahead of them down the plushly-carpeted corridors. This was evidently the top-class section of the big hotel. The porter stopped in front of a big mahogany double-door, fished a key out of his pocket, and ushered them humbly into the chambers within. Sighing inwardly, Storm followed Jason.

'Oh, my God!'

She followed Jason's incredulous gaze to the bed. The bed? It was a modern hotelier's notion of a throne of love—an unbelievably vast and ornate structure over-hung with a silk-tasselled canopy. The expansive head-board curved in rococo arabesques, forming a large pink-plush-padded heart in the centre. Little gilt cupids aimed arrows from each of the four corners. Around the decorated edge of the divan, muscular nymphs chased busty shepherdesses through woodland glades. And this incredible bed was very obviously the centrepiece of the room. Everything else—small, coy chairs and dressing-tables, a sprinkling of coffee-tables and sofas—was arranged around it. There was little doubt as to what the hotel expected a honeymoon couple's priorities to be. Storm was unable to suppress a giggle at the ghastliness of it, and Jason glared at her. The obsequious porter allowed himself one respectful but undeniably salacious

wink, pocketed Jason's tip, and closed the door behind
him.

With another appalled glance at the bed, Jason
pushed through the interleading door. A small break-
fast-room was revealed, its big glass doors leading on to
a balcony. They walked through into the by now cold
night air, and gazed down at the brilliantly illuminated
city below.

'Well,' volunteered Storm, 'at least the bed's big
enough to give us ten square feet each.'

'I'm surprised it hasn't got mirrors in the ceiling,' said
Jason sourly.

'Oh, it has,' she smiled. 'You simply pull one of the
cords, and the curtains come open.' Colour rose to her
cheeks under Jason's hard stare. 'I just happened to
notice,' she finished in a small voice.

'Clever you,' he grunted, then stretched his big shoulders. 'Want to go down and see the sights for an hour
before we climb into the Good Ship Venus?' he asked
laconically.

The Piazza Maggiore was ablaze with excitement. The
orchestra had redoubled their efforts, and were now
thumping out a selection of Franz Léhar's operetta
numbers, the romantic hits of eighty years ago. A
sprinkling of snow hadn't dampened anyone's ardour
noticeably, and the tree-lined square was whirling with
dancing couples. Jason had bought Storm a box of
Cremona candies—exquisite roasted almonds coated in
crisp sugar, truffles redolent with rum, brandy-snaps
filled with bewilderingly delicious cream—and she was
polishing them off with wide-eyed relish, one hand

tucked under his arm, against the hard muscles of his side.

'Is this snow going to make any difference?' she wanted to know.

'What—to our honeymoon night?'

'No,' she said, embarrassed, 'to the race.'

'Probably not. If it gets too heavy, we can always rise above the clouds. The snow will just make everything prettier. The sponsors probably have an arrangement with the Almighty.'

She smiled at his irreverence. A couple at a nearby table rose to leave, and Jason tugged her over to it, and they sat down to watch the dancing. A beaming waiter brought them coffee and Grappa—a form of liquid fire—and they drank the warming beverages gratefully.

'Want to dance?' he asked with a smile.

She shook her head.

'No, thanks, if you don't mind. I'll just sit here and relax. Hasn't it been—'

'*Ciao, bello!*' The coal-eyed beauty who had kissed Jason through the Fiat's window appeared through the crowd, her pretty red mouth smiling. Utterly ignoring Storm, she perched herself on the table next to Jason.

'*Ciao, bella,*' he smiled.

'*Vuoi ballare?*'

'She wants me to dance,' he explained to Storm, peering round the girl's adolescent bottom.

'I know,' she replied shortly. 'I've got a degree in Italian.'

Impatient, the girl took Jason's hand and hauled him out of the chair.

'I'll be back in a minute,' he grinned.

'Take your time,' Storm told him sourly, and smiled

with murder in her heart. The girl whisked Jason into the thick of the dancers. The last she saw of them was a red-nailed hand sliding possessively across his back.

She sat in silent fury. Wasn't it Italian *men* who were supposed to be so forward? She lost sight of them in the crowd. She had let herself in for a very special kind of torture, that was obvious. What a pity that she couldn't have been cool, hard-headed Storm, the way she had wanted to be! How exciting this trip would have been—if only she hadn't had the bad sense to fall in love with Jason Bentley! Or *was* it love? The spasms of jealousy that had racked her when the Italian girl had whisked Jason away were, after all, perfectly natural. Any woman would have felt annoyed at having her partner spirited away under her nose. Was it really a deep emotion, this feeling she had for Jason?

Maybe it was just infatuation. A delayed schoolgirl crush. She recalled the passion she had felt for her first-year tutor, poor moth-eaten old Mr Derbyshire. That had blown over soon enough. Maybe this would, too. No, it wasn't love. It couldn't be! If it had really been love, she would have made Jason see it by now. If it was really love, surely they—*Damn!* There was that *blasted* girl again! Storm narrowed green eyes furiously. Look at her—clinging to him like that, pert little teenage breasts pressed against his chest. Shameless hussy! Where was her mother? She watched Jason's splendid face smiling down into the girl's, his white teeth glinting in his smile. She laughed, a delicious gurgle that came to Storm over the hubbub of the crowd. Jason waved, catching sight of her. Storm pretended not to have noticed, and stared grimly in the opposite direction. It certainly wasn't love—that was for sure. It was simply a passing infatuation. She stared glumly at Jason's untouched glass of Grappa. No wonder all those Borgia women had carried poison pills hidden in their rings!

Even the bathroom at the Imperial had been designed with the theoretical insatiable honeymoon couple in mind. The gilt towel-rings were labelled HIS and HERS, and the bath was a vast purple ceramic orchid, obviously made for conjugal bathing. The plethora of mirrors everywhere was calculated, Storm thought sourly, to pander to the narcissism of the newly-wedded couple, who would no doubt be prancing around in the buff most of the time, tottering from the champagne trolley to that astoundingly suggestive bed.

Storm glared at her sensible-nightie-clad form in the mirror. The *swine!* She hadn't spoken to him on the way back to the hotel—once that little hussy had finally been prised away from him by her friends. And there was still a smear of her nasty lipstick (a sickly colour, no doubt called *Cupid's Toes*) on his chin. Storm brushed her even teeth with venomous energy, spewed Colgate into the orchid-shaped basin, and stamped through into the bedroom. Jason was already in bed, his magnificent naked torso propped up against the pillows, reading a book. And a new horror was revealed—the sheets were made of gold silk! Not passionate scarlet or decadent black—but gold. His tawny eyes met hers, dropped to her ankle-length nightie, then returned to his book. It really was the most embarrassing situation Storm had ever been in. She stalked over to the dressing-table and began brushing her gleaming hair in the mirror. She could see him in it, the crisp dark curls covering his muscular chest. His wide shoulders and arms were rocky with muscle. It was an athlete's body, hard and virile. She tore her eyes away from him, her stomach suddenly hollow and trembling. Was she really going to have to climb into that bed with him? With Jason in it, it suddenly didn't look farcical at all. Against the golden sheets, his body was magnificent, a beautiful rich colour—

'Don't brush it all off,' he requested drily, looking up at her with cool eyes. Storm put the brush down with gritted teeth and walked over to the bed, her heart in her throat. She slipped under the covers; the mattress was deliciously soft and firm. No doubt designed by experts to give the best results for—well, never mind. She turned her back on him ostentatiously, and snuggled down among the soft pillows, squeezing her eyes shut.

'Is anything wrong?' he asked quietly.

'Wrong?' she asked with elaborate surprise. 'Of course not. What should be wrong?'

'You just seem a bit tense, that's all.'

She heard him turn a page, and there was a silence. She lay, about as relaxed as a cat sleeping next to a dog, and thought about all the cutting things she would like to say to him—if he gave her the chance.

'You're not upset about that child, are you?'

'What child?' she asked in the same surprised voice.

There was another pause.

'Anyway,' she said, her voice muffled by the pillow, 'if she was a child, then I'm a grandmother.'

A strong hand clamped on her shoulder and hauled her round to face cool eyes.

'What did you say?' Jason demanded.

'I said she wasn't a child,' Storm repeated, looking up rebelliously into his face, her hands clutching the coverlet.

'She was fifteen,' he retorted.

'Yes? The way she was dancing, you wouldn't have thought so.'

He stared down at her, his eyes deep and thoughtful.

'You look rather gorgeous against these sheets,' he said inconsequentially. Storm's heart turned over as he reached out, and brushed the soft hair away from her face. 'As a matter of fact,' he said gently, 'you look rather gorgeous anywhere.' She stared up at him, fascinated by him. God, he was so beautiful! If only she could reach out and claim that big, male body for her own! If only they really *were* on honeymoon!

'In less than two days' time, you and I are going to be in the air together,' he said. His smile rocked her, and she nodded, her throat too dry to answer. He stroked her hair gently back, a caress that made her want to melt against him. The warm presence of his body, so close to hers that she could sense it with every nerve in her skin, was beginning to make her feel rather giddy. Maybe that was what altitude did to you?

'Storm,' he said quietly, his eyes warm and caressing on hers, 'I'm beginning to think I've treated you harshly over the past few days.'

Harshly? Oh no, darling—you only took six layers of my skin off . . . Aloud, Storm said, 'You've been under a strain—I understand.'

'Do you? You've helped a lot, Storm. I don't exactly know how—but having you around has made things easier for me.'

'I'm glad,' she said in a small voice. Jason leaned over,

and she closed her eyes for his kiss, her heart racing. It landed with brotherly affection on her forehead.

'Let's get some sleep, okay? Goodnight, little one.'

'Goodnight,' she whispered. *Little one!* The affection in that endearment was some consolation for the disappointment of his kiss. She curled up, aware that her insides had melted, that an all-too-familiar ache had started up in her tummy. Jason examined the panel of switches next to the bed in some perplexity.

'It's like the console of the Starship Enterprise,' he muttered, and flicked a switch experimentally. Instantly, the sweet sound of gypsy violins drifted from concealed speakers.

'This damned thing was designed for very unimaginative couples,' he commented sourly, and Storm giggled. He tried another switch. The main lights went off, but the bed was now bathed in sensuous pink light. They stared at each other. The effect was like a Turkish bordello from the eighteen-eighties. Grimly, Jason tried again. The pink was replaced by ultra-violet light, a deep purple glow in which their teeth shone fluorescent white, their bodies outlined starkly against the golden sheets. Jason muttered something unprintable, and Storm giggled again.

'Is this what honeymoon couples have to go through?' he enquired drily. 'God help them—as if they haven't got enough troubles of their own! I'm afraid to touch anything else in case we get launched into outer space.'

'Let me try,' she smiled, and leaned over him to press the buttons. For brief seconds a strobe-light flashed mercilessly, then the room was plunged into soft darkness. And Storm suddenly became aware that she was lying across Jason's hard, naked chest. She looked into his eyes. And then his arms came around her, imprisoning her there before she could slide away.

'You weren't really jealous of that girl, were you?' he asked, his eyes glinting in the darkness. She could smell him, a mixture of aftershave, man, and warm skin.

'Of course I wasn't,' she said, trying to keep her voice level. Through her nightie, his body was firm and warm. 'I—I just didn't like being left on my own, that's all.'

'Tell me the truth,' he said gently. 'You're not getting any silly notions about me, are you? No romantic delusions, I mean?'

'Certainly not!' she denied, glad of the darkness that hid her hot cheeks.

'I meant what I said that night at my father's place,' he reminded her. 'Helena Salisbury cured me of any desire to engage in romantic delusions of my own, Storm. I'm simply not interested.'

'Nor am I,' she assured him, trying to sound sincere.

'Are you sure?' he enquired. 'No silly flutterings of the heart?'

'None,' she gritted, acutely aware of his powerful chest under her palms, wishing he'd let her go. It was becoming increasingly difficult to hold herself away from him—her whole being was yearning for him, longing to dissolve against him, be protected by his power, surrender to his strength. 'None at all.'

'Good,' he purred. And pulled her to him, his lips finding hers with shocking intimacy, probing the moistness of her mouth. 'Have you changed your mind about letting me make love to you?' he murmured.

'*No!*' she gasped.

His smile was lazy, supremely confident.

'Sure?' He kissed her eyes, sealing them shut, and

cradled her head against his cheek. 'I want you, Storm. You know that, don't you?'

'Yes,' she whispered.

'Come and lie in my arms.' With irresistible strength, he pulled her across his body so that she was lying curled against the hardness of him, her head resting on the firm pillow of his shoulder. 'I can feel your heart beating,' he told her softly. 'Are you afraid of me?'

'In some ways,' she admitted, her lips close against his skin. She could feel the length of his body against hers. He was naked except for briefs, and she was scaldingly aware of the thinness of her nightie—all that was preventing their skins from touching. His hand brushed the roundness of her hip, moved down her thigh, slipped under the hem of her nightgown . . .

'In what ways are you afraid of me?' he prompted softly. Storm gasped silently as his hand caressed the flinching skin of her thigh, stroking her hip, then the tenderness of her flanks.

'This is what I'm afraid of,' she said in a shaking voice. 'What you can do to me—what I let you do to me!'

'Don't you want it?'

'No,' she moaned, tasting the tang of his skin with her tongue, wanting to bite the firm flesh, 'it would be so wrong, Jason—'

'But if there's no emotional tangle, what could be wrong about it?' he asked, his hand brushing over the plane of her stomach and down to her silky thighs.

Emotional tangle! Storm shut her eyes, her heart torn in half. Dear Heaven, what could be more bitterly ironic? His touch was maddening, dissolving her will to resist; it was becoming a sweet torment that threatened to make her call out.

'You don't understand,' she gasped.

'But I do,' he answered, his own voice rough with desire. His caress was coming closer and closer to fulfilling the ache of her desire; and yet the closer it got, the fiercer he made her ache.

'Doesn't morality mean anything to you?' she begged. She stopped his hand desperately. 'Jason, please tell me about her.'

'About who?' he asked, puzzled.

'Helena Salisbury. Did she—did she hurt you very badly?'

'I suppose so,' he said impatiently. 'Why do you want to know?'

'Then—you must have loved her very much,' she ventured in a small voice.

Jason sighed explosively, and lay back.

'Helena's a socialite, Storm. One of the beautiful people. I guess I was infatuated with her for a while, yes—more fool me. She was utterly shallow—a person who cared for nothing except her clothes and her figure, and what other people thought of her. Forget her, Storm.'

'Yet,' she murmured, 'men often love women like that very deeply.'

'Are you asking me if I still feel anything for Helena Salisbury?' He shook his head slowly. 'I don't, Storm. Not in that way, I promise.'

'You remember the hurt, though,' she accused. 'If you're still hurt by what she did, then you must still love her!'

'I never loved her, Storm,' he grated. 'I never even pretended to. And it was her betrayal which hurt me—not the conclusion of our affair. Believe me.' His lips found hers again, teasing, tormenting, until she strained towards him, no longer caring whether she was the first or the last woman in his arms, no longer caring whether he still felt anything for Helena Salisbury. It took a massive effort of will to resist the deep urge in her to give in to him, to let him take her, however he wanted.

'If you ask me to stop, I will,' he whispered. His skin was burning against her; it was as though every muscle in her body was melting, aching to flood into him, become one with him. 'If you don't tell me to stop,' he said, 'then I won't, Storm. I need you so much—I need your gentleness, your comfort . . .' His words were setting her on fire almost more than his touch. Restlessly, she slid her hand down the smooth, hard plane of his stomach. His reaction was instantaneous, a deep gasp of passion that set her pulses racing. Oh no! Was her own body rebelling against her? Jason's skin was damp against her, his breath coming in light pants. Storm's own feelings were becoming too much for her to bear. Desperately she closed her mind to her own doubts, to caution, to that last instinct of self-preservation that was screaming *he'll break your heart* inside her. Her face pressed against his chest, his heart pounding against her cheek, she slid her fingers timidly across his body, her heart delighting fiercely in the deep moan that broke from his lips—

The sound of the telephone was a squeal that slashed through the nerve-melting silence of their passion. They both froze in disbelief and horror as the strident sound shrilled in the darkness. And Storm, her mind fluttering down to earth, breathed a prayer of relief. With a curse, Jason snapped the night-light on, sat up angrily, his beautiful torso covered in a sheen of sweat, and picked up the receiver. He took a deep breath, and in the calmest voice he could muster, said, 'Yes?'

She lay back, feeling slightly dizzy, her whole body aching with unquenched desire, and watched the man she loved so very much as he listened to the voice on the other end. His tawny eyes widened, his mouth tugging into a wry grimace. He let the receiver drop into his lap and stared at her in disbelief.

'It's the manager,' he told her, his voice husky. 'He says he's managed to find two single rooms, and do we want them now?'

CHAPTER SEVEN

THE balloon arrived the next morning, air-freight from Milan. Most of the day was taken up getting it ready for the race, which was to begin the next morning at seven-thirty sharp. The starting post, so to speak, was the beautiful big field just outside the city called the Campo Graziano. Leaving Jason to make all the pre-race checks to the instruments and the burner, Storm wandered through the big crowd of balloonists engaged in similar occupations to a mobile hot-dog stand to get them both a snack.

It was easy to see why this had been called 'The Race of the Falling Leaves'. The countryside had just begun to turn into its full autumn colouring—and it was breath-takingly lovely. Under a cool, clear sky, the trees were a thousand different russet shades, amber and rust and yellow and red. The grass was dotted with the last flowers of summer and the first flowers of autumn, and covered with a light, crisp layer of leaves. As she stood waiting for her hot-dog, the light breeze shook a little shower of drying leaves out of the row of poplars.

'*Bel tempo*,' smiled the hot-dog man, charmed with this beautiful blonde with the warm green eyes. Storm rewarded him with a smile. It was indeed beautiful weather. A beautiful time of the year, in fact—you could feel nature hovering between one season and the next, a moment of stillness before the voluptuousness of full summer gave way to the graver beauty of autumn.

132

The Campo Graziano was thronged with people, the vast majority of them enthusiastic onlookers. The balloons themselves were mostly spread out over the lush grass, swathes of brightly-coloured polyurethane; but one or two of the competitors had inflated their craft experimentally, and the gigantic spheres hung over the busy scene, swaying majestically in the gentle wind. The camera crews of various international television companies were vying for the best angles, and as Storm bore her hot-dogs back to Jason through the crowd, she passed the white bus of the B.B.C. crew.

'You're English, aren't you?' asked one of the cameramen, and when Storm nodded, wanted to know whether she was joining the race. His eyes lighting up, he summoned the interviewer on his walkie-talkie.

'We've been looking for Bentley everywhere,' he informed her. 'Will he give us an interview, do you think?'

'You could try,' she smiled, and led them through the crowds to where Jason was untangling the rigging of the crimson-and-turquoise balloon.

The interview began routinely enough. Storm, surprisingly unexcited by her first contact with the mass media, watched Jason's handsome face as he answered the interviewer's questions crisply and fluently.

'So you think you've got a chance of winning?' demanded the reporter, a thin-faced man from the Sports team.

'Certainly,' said Jason, showing his perfect teeth in a grin that was going, Storm thought wryly, to set a million hearts fluttering in Britain. The interviewer turned back to the cameras.

'Jason Bentley, of course, is better known as one of Britain's most ambitious young barristers. Most viewers will recall him as the defending lawyer in the notorious Cannon Street murder case.' He turned back to Jason, whose tawny eyes were narrowing ominously. 'Getting Morgan and Outram acquitted was quite a feather in your cap, wasn't it, Mr Bentley?' The sneer in the man's voice was not quite concealed, and Jason shrugged angrily. Storm's heart sank. Nothing would please this reporter better than to get Jason Bentley to explode in front of the cameras, which she could see were moving to take close-ups of Jason's face.

'I suppose you've been very busy with the preparations for this race,' the interviewer pursued with a smile like a razor. 'I wonder if you've heard that Mavis Walker, the prosecution's chief witness, was brutally murdered in a Soho club a few days after the trial?'

'Yes,' Jason grated, 'I'm quite aware of that fact.' His brown hands had balled into fists. The interviewer could obviously sense Jason's tension, and licked his thin lips.

'I suppose you were very pleased with yourself when you secured the release of Billy Morgan and Butch Outram,' he continued, 'even though you knew—'

'It's my job,' said Jason, his eyes like ice. Storm's heart was pounding. She knew what was coming. This interviewer was going to get his explosion, no matter how; and Jason's inner agony over the case was going to blind him to reason—until it was too late.

'Of course it's your job,' sneered the reporter. 'And a most indispensable job, too. Still, getting those boys off that charge doesn't seem to have done Mavis Walker any good, does it?'

'That's libellous!' Jason snapped, his powerful body rigid with tension.

'Is it?' The reporter's narrow eyebrows arched skyward. 'Why? I haven't said anything naughty, have I?'

'You've damn near implied that Morgan and Outram killed Mavis Walker!' Jason snarled. His temper was clearly slipping, and Storm groaned inwardly. This was going to be a disaster!

'You don't think they did?' enquired the reporter nastily.

'It has nothing to do with me,' he retorted, his mouth a hard line.

'No?' Again, the thin eyebrows expressed disbelief. The reporter changed tack. 'Constable Davis was buried last Wednesday,' he said. 'He was twenty-five.'

'It's very tragic,' Jason gritted.

'Yes, isn't it?' jeered the reporter, sensing that Jason was going to lose his temper any minute now. 'But Constable Davis's killers have escaped scot-free—'

'They haven't been arrested yet,' Jason interrupted, his face hard and angry.

The reporter jeered, 'A lot of people think they *were* arrested, Mr Bentley—and that you were clever enough to get them off!'

'Outram and Morgan didn't kill that policeman,' he snarled in reply.

'No? But then, you've been paid very well to prove that, haven't you?' the interviewer retorted offensively.

'Damn you—' Jason began, stepping forwards with clenched fists. Desperately, Storm grabbed his arm and tugged him possessively to her.

'You don't seem to have much knowledge of English law,' she told the reporter with a bright smile. The cameras jumped to her, and the reporter, his prize apparently snatched away for the time being, held out the microphone sourly.

'What do you mean by that, Miss—er—Calderwood?'

'I mean that the case in question is over and done with. And Morgan and Outram were acquitted of the murder of P.C. Davis. That means,' she added, as though explaining some simple point to a very small child, 'that they were found innocent. Not guilty as charged.'

'Yes, but—'

'They were tried by jury,' she reminded him calmly. 'A group of twelve adult men and women—who had no axe to grind, and no expectations either way. And they decided that Morgan and Outram didn't do it. So,' she concluded, looking at him with cool green eyes, 'for you to start insinuating that they were guilty after all is not only ridiculous—it's despicable.'

Jason stood silent, his eyes still narrowed. The reporter gulped, then ventured a sour smile.

'Morgan and Outram happen to be a pair of thugs—'

'No one's denying that,' Storm interrupted calmly. 'But it happens to be another fundamental point of English law that people are only charged with one thing at a time. And no matter what these two kids had done at other times, they didn't kill P.C. Davis. And it would have been a gross miscarriage of justice for them to have been convicted.'

'But Mavis Walker—'

'Her death is also tragic,' Storm nodded. 'But her evidence during the trial was proved to be malicious and totally false.'

The reporter looked nonplussed.

'That doesn't mean she deserved what happened to her,' he said at last.

'Of course not—that would be a terrible thing to say. But it's equally terrible to try and blame Jason Bentley for her death—when it seems to me that he's acted superbly throughout what was an extremely difficult and ambiguous case.'

There was a silence, filled by the distant sound of a public address system blaring out the weather reports. The interviewer smiled thinly at them both.

'Well, Mr Bentley,' he commented, 'it seems you've got yourself a very effective defence lawyer of your own. I'm sorry if I—'

One of the technicians had edged up to him, his headphones still in place, holding out a copy of the previous day's *Telegraph*. There were pictures of Billy Morgan and Mavis Walker on the front page, and the technician tapped the article underneath. 'Better read that, Sam,' he suggested. The reporter ran through the article with careful eyes as the cameramen relaxed, lowering their heavy machines and lighting cigarettes.

'Butch Outram's shopped Billy Morgan,' he commented. 'He's being charged with the murder of Mavis Walker.'

'Let me see that.' Jason took the paper, and raced through the article. The reporter looked at Storm.

'Their alibi collapsed,' he told her. 'And what's more, they've identified the real killers of Constable Davis—three heavies from one of the East End gangs. They've been arrested, too. It's quite a breakthrough for the police.'

Jason looked up with thoughtful eyes.

'I knew it,' he muttered.

The reporter wiped his chin, then smiled.

'Mr Bentley, it seems I owe you an apology. Your defence lawyer,' he gestured at Storm, 'was right after all. You made the right decision in a very difficult situation. I'm sorry for the things I said.'

'It's your job,' Jason shrugged, giving him a wry smile.

'Yeah—but I was doing it a little too well. Look, can we do this interview again? Right from the top?'

Jason hesitated, then nodded.

'Terrific—and no bull this time, I promise. Miss Calderwood, will you move up again and take his arm, like you did before? Okay, that's great. What a handsome couple, eh, boys?'

Storm grinned up at Jason as the clapperboard snapped, and then the reporter was leaning forward with professional charm.

'Brilliant lawyer Jason Bentley has a rather unusual hobby,' he began. 'When he's not ensuring that justice is done in rainy London, he's out here in Italy, competing in one of the world's most glamorous and prestigious races—the Trans-Alps Balloon Race, more familiarly known as the Race of the Falling Leaves . . .'

As the camera crew moved off, their interview done, Storm rather timidly held out the by now cold hot-dog she had been clutching ever since she had arrived back from the stand.

'It's gone a bit soggy,' she apologised. 'Want me to get you another one?'

Jason stared at her for long seconds, his eyes unfathomable. Then he took the hot-dog, tossed it away, and took Storm's face in both his hands. The kiss he planted on her lips was the most forceful and thorough kiss she had ever known.

'Wow,' she said shakily.

He smiled.

'Thanks—Portia.'

'Portia?'

'Never mind.' He patted her cheek. 'You seem to have changed your views about my profession,' he added drily. 'Anyway, you got me out of a lot of hot water back there. I was just about to knock friend Sam flat.'

'I know,' she said, still pink from his kiss. She avoided his eyes. 'Is the balloon ready yet?'

'Just about. There's a little trouble with the altimeter. It won't take me more than a few minutes to sort out, and then we'll go back to Cremona for lunch. Okay?'

She nodded, and stood back to watch him work on the delicate instrument with sure fingers. Her lips still felt bruised after his kiss, and her thoughts instinctively turned to the night before. Her blush stayed in place as she recalled the huge bed, how close she had come to giving in to him. After that providential phone call, they had both laughed until they were weak, the manager's voice an enquiring squawk from the abandoned receiver on the coverlet. Then she had curled up in Jason's strong arms and gone to sleep at once—to awake the next morning with her face against his chest and her hand upon the flat plane of his stomach.

'What are you thinking about?' She blinked. Jason hadn't looked up to ask the question, but was carefully arranging what looked like a watch-spring in a little metal cylinder.

'Nothing in particular,' she lied.

He slid the cylinder home with a click, and looked up at her.

'I enjoyed last night,' he said quietly.

'Oh—' Her blush had returned.

'And I don't mean just the hanky-panky, either,' he rebuked her.

'What, then?'

'Sleeping with you. Literally.' He stood up, dusting his hands, and Storm was suddenly reminded of the first time she had met him. He had dusted his hands with exactly the same movement then, too. 'Being with you. You're very restful, Storm.'

'Am I?'

'Not when you focus those green eyes on me in a certain way,' he admitted. 'But in general—yes. There's something deeply peaceful in you, Storm.'

'There is?' She gaped at him. 'My friends have always told me what a restless person I am, never able to stay in one place for two minutes—'

'Not any more.'

'What?'

He smiled gently at her. 'Can't you tell? You've changed, Storm. Probably for ever.'

She stared into his tawny eyes, thinking about what he had said.

'Do you mean that?' she asked.

'Look at yourself—I don't mean physically. You're different—much calmer, more balanced. Less inclined to be stupid and upset. The Storm I met two weeks ago would never have been able to deal with that reporter as cleverly as you did. You seem to know your own mind so much better now, too.'

He was right. She had grown up over the past weeks more rapidly than in the past few years. And she did know her mind now. She knew that she loved Jason Bentley more than words could tell. And that he didn't love her.

'Looking forward to the ball tonight?' he asked casually, pulling on his anorak.

'The ball?'

'Wake up, dozey,' he said drily. 'We're going to the competitors' ball to-night—remember?'

'Oh. Yes, I remember. And I'm looking forward to it very much,' she said slowly.

Jason looked at her.

'You could have fooled me,' he commented.

The ball itself was a grand affair, held in the Baroque city hall. In addition to the hundred and twenty competitors, there were at least twice as many newspeople, race officials, civic dignitaries (looking unbelievably solemn in their robes of office) and guests of honour. These last included a famous and beautiful Italian actress who had been brought in to lend her aura to the general atmosphere. Storm and Jason had been seated at her table, among a glittering arrangement of roses, silver and crystal, and she had been admiring the star all night. Enviously, Storm noted the older woman's flawless skin and incredibly long, but obviously natural, eyelashes. That famous face, she reflected, was at least fifty years old now; yet the years had only added grace and ineffable beauty to the fabulous figure, the big, lustrous eyes, the wide, mysteriously smiling mouth.

'Isn't she stunning?' Storm whispered to Jason. 'She's like a queen!'

'Yes. And when she started, she was only a Neapolitan flower-girl.' He smiled as they watched the great lady listening with gracious interest to some long-winded story the mayor was telling.

'I'd give anything to be as beautiful as she is,' Storm whispered enviously.

'You're more beautiful than she ever was,' Jason told her quietly.

She looked at him, wide-eyed. 'What?' She blinked, then looked away. 'Oh, you're just being kind to me—'

'Why should I be kind to you?' He surveyed her gravely, a splendid figure in magnificent evening dress. 'It's true. She's a hothouse beauty, but you—you're fresh, natural. I don't think I've ever known a woman who was lovelier than you, Storm.'

She gaped at him, feeling slightly giddy. Was he serious? Before she could stammer out a reply, the mayor's story had reached its unfunny conclusion, and the great star was leaning over to Jason, her lustrous eyes interested.

'And you, *signore*, do you also intend to win the race?'

'Of course, *madama*,' he smiled. 'There isn't any other philosophy, is there?'

'Not for you men,' answered the star, her eyes sparkling. 'For us poor women it is different, no? We must languish at home while you big strong creatures go out and win races, build canals, make wars. Am I not correct?'

'You are too modest, *madama*,' Jason grinned. 'Look what carnage you've wrought.'

'I?' she purred, her eyes half-closing.

'You, *madama*—im masculine hearts across the globe.'

She laughed, a delicious chuckle that bubbled from the slender column of her throat.

'But my victims do not actually die, *signore*!'

'Not once, no—a thousand times!'

She laughed again. The mayor, smiling blandly, cleared his throat as the prelude to yet another endless tale, and the great star raised her eyes heavenwards for a split second—a tiny plea for rescue, intended for Jason alone.

'Would you do me the honour of dancing with me, *madama*?'

'I should be enchanted,' she purred, turning the full force of her almond eyes on Storm. 'That is—if your beautiful partner has no objections?'

'None, *madama*,' Storm answered with good grace, and watched as they walked arm-in-arm on to the floor. The band raced into the Blue Danube Waltz in honour of the actress, and suddenly the dance floor was thronged with couples waltzing gaily underneath the vast red helium balloon that the organisers had suspended over the floor. Storm watched Jason and the actress, so splendidly matched, as they moved among the crowd. Was she destined to spend the whole of her time in Italy sitting out while Jason danced with the female population of Italy? Her heart ached for him. Did he really think her beautiful? Or was he simply being kind to a little English girl miles from home?

A profound melancholy settled on her. Tomorrow the race would be under way. They would spend some hectic hours together, high above the clouds—and then they would be back in England, separating. Would she ever see Jason again, once the race was done? She doubted it. He had warned her not to have any romantic expectations—and she had ignored him. But could she have helped it? Could anyone help falling in love? She recalled the way it had come to her, so abruptly, in the kitchenette of her little flat, and smiled sadly. The waltz was racing to its joyful climax, and Jason was whirling the actress in his arms as though she were a feather. With a burst of applause, the waltz was over, and the band were rushing into *The Rose of Istanbul*. Jason led his partner, flushed and smiling her famous smile, back to the table. The mayor and his entourage were ready to receive her, and Jason sat down with Storm again, turning to her with a grin.

'Want to—' He stopped, looking at her. She was close to tears. He leaned forward. 'Do you want to go home?' he asked quietly. Storm nodded, and at once he rose, drawing her up, and led her through the crowded tables to the exit. At the cloakroom she collected her beautiful white coat, and they made their way into the cool night air. While they had been in the ballroom, it had been snowing unnoticed, and Cremona was covered in a fine, white layer of crisp snow. Jason's arm was around her waist, and she leaned her head miserably on his shoulder. The doorman whistled for a taxi as they came out, but Jason shook his head abruptly, and walked Storm down the marble stairs into the street, and across the poplar-lined square. She pulled the wool of her coat closer around her thin silk gown.

'Where are we going?' she asked.

'To get a carriage home,' he smiled.

'A carriage?'

He had walked her to other side of the square, where the old quarter of the city lay. A row of open horse-carriages stood in the quiet street, waiting for custom. The snow was still drifting down gently, and the big chestnut horses steamed and stamped softly in the crisp air.

'This is how people used to go home from balls,' Jason

smiled. 'These old chaps are the last of a dying breed.'

The leading cabby, seeing them coming towards him, urged his horse into a trot, and met them on the corner of the square.

'The Imperial, please,' Jason instructed him, and helped Storm into the carriage. The seats were of red leather, polished smooth by years of use, and there were several travelling rugs in one corner. Jason wrapped Storm's slender legs in one, tucking it in behind her, then sat back on the seat opposite with one arm along the back.

The little silver bells on the carriage jingled musically, and the clop-clop of the horse's hooves was a delicious, old-fashioned sound that echoed quietly along the empty, snow-filled streets. Storm lay back, the snowflakes drifting like tiny cool kisses on to her face, and breathed in the night air. It smelled vaguely of chestnuts roasting, and fresh snow.

'Now,' said Jason calmly, 'what's it all about, Storm?'

'What's what about?' she fenced, avoiding his eyes.

'You. When I got back from that dance, you looked as though you were going to burst into tears. What is it?'

'Nothing,' she sighed. 'I'm just getting a bit emotional, that's all.'

'About the race?' he asked carefully. She nodded, and he seemed to relax slightly. The movement of the carriage was infinitely soothing, a gentle rocking motion that for some reason reminded Storm of her childhood. 'What a lovely idea this was,' she said, forcing a smile.

'I'm glad you like it,' he said, but his tawny eyes were watchful. The cabby, an ancient top hat tilted back on his grizzled head, clucked encouragingly to his horse.

Cremona was a silent city, its streets almost deserted. Only when they passed a café or a tavern did they hear the sound of festivity, and catch sight of happy crowds through the lighted windows. And the snow drifted down imperceptibly. They rode in silence, Storm watching his face covertly, aching with her love for him. At the Imperial, they went straight up to their room without speaking. Picking up the telephone, Jason ordered coffee and a light snack—neither of them had eaten at the ball—and they sat down in the chintz armchairs, both quiet.

'It's not just the race, is it?' Jason asked gently.

Storm opened her mouth to protest, saw the look in his eyes, and shut her mouth.

'Yes,' she said at last. 'It's more than the race.'

'What is it, then? Me?'

'Yes,' she whispered. The waiter brought their coffee in with a tray of open sandwiches and some fruit, and they watched him put it down and bow himself out in silence. Jason poured coffee, passed her her cup, then sat back, his eyes grave.

'Storm,' he began gently, 'I once warned you against getting any silly romantic notions about me.'

'Why are they silly?' she demanded, comforting her hands on the warmth of the coffee-cup.

'Because you'll only get hurt, Storm. You should have settled for a purely physical relationship.'

'Jason, I—'

'It would have been healthier and easier for us both,' he said brutally. 'Romantic infatuations are only going to get in our way.'

'In the way of your damned race, you mean,' she flared. 'Is that all you ever think about?'

'It's the reason we're here,' he reminded her coldly.

'I'm not a machine, Jason,' she said bitterly. 'I didn't want this to happen, either.'

'Look,' he said shortly, 'to be quite frank—you didn't have much of an idea about sex before you met me, did you?'

'You know I didn't,' she said sullenly.

'Exactly. And for the first time, you've met a man who's older than you are, and who knows a bit more about sex than you. What you've experienced with me is just desire, Storm. After all, you're a healthy young woman—it's perfectly natural. It's sex, pure and simple, not some huge emotional discovery.'

'That's what you'd like to think,' she said angrily.

'I wanted someone to help me with this bloody race,' he retorted. 'Not someone to get in my way!'

'How have I been in your way?' she demanded.

Jason stood up restlessly, and paced the room.

'Do you think I enjoy being with you?' he snapped. 'Do you think it's easy being with a beautiful woman, sleeping in the same bed with her, sharing your life with her—and not being allowed to touch?'

'You've touched plenty,' she reminded him acidly.

'I want to make love to you,' he rasped. 'Not to—to play virgin's games all night!'

'Make love to me, then,' she whispered, her heart thudding.

He pulled a scornful face. 'Don't try and act the whore, Storm, because you're not one.'

'I'm not acting,' she said in a strained voice. She let the white coat slip away from her shoulders, revealing the golden skin of her arms and throat against the blue of her gown. He clenched his teeth, his eyes crossing her body hungrily, then turned away.

'Stop it, Storm,' he grated.

'Do you think I don't want you?' she whispered. 'And if you just want my body, Jason, then I've made my mind up at last. Take me—'

'For God's sake grow up,' he snapped. 'You don't think I'd have anything to do with you now, do you?'

'Why not? Just because—'

'Because you've chosen to fill your idiotic young head with sentimental trash, that's why,' he said grimly.

'I know what Helena Salisbury did to you,' she said urgently, 'but you can't base the rest of your life on your feelings about her!'

'Helena?' he snorted. 'I don't give a damn about Helena any more—you're presenting me with enough problems on your own, young lady.'

'Am I?' she asked, not knowing whether to be pleased or not by what he had said. 'Then why don't you try and solve some of them—right now?' she said provocatively.

'Not as long as your brain is addled with romantic flummery,' he retorted.

'Why keep calling it silly romantic this and sentimental that?' she demanded. 'It does have a name, you know.'

'Love?' he scorned. 'Not likely!'

'Why not?' she asked quietly.

'Because I'm too old for you, for one thing,' he said roughly.

'You're only ten years older—'

'I'm a thousand years older in experience,' he interrupted.

'Then show me,' she pleaded. His eyes blazed, and he

strode over to her, gripping the arms of her chair with white-knuckled fingers.

'Can't you see I'm aching to?' he said passionately. 'Can't you see how much I want you, want to touch you, crush you against me?'

'Jason—' She reached out trembling hands to caress his face. 'Darling—'

'Storm, I don't want to hurt you,' he groaned. 'I need you so very much—but not in the way you want—'

'In what way, then?'

'Like this.' His kiss was fierce, passionate, his arms tight around her shoulders. He picked her up in his arms and stared down at her with eyes that intoxicated and thrilled. 'God,' he muttered roughly, 'I'd like to lay you down on that bed now and make love to you!'

She clung to his neck. 'If that's what you want, then take me,' she breathed.

He shook his head, his eyes tormented.

'If you just wanted what I want, it would be so easy,' he said quietly. He carried her over to the bed and laid her gently on it. She clung to his arms as he stared down at her beautiful face, smoothing her golden hair out over the coverlet.

'Oh, Storm,' he sighed, caressing her face lightly, 'why do this to me?'

'I mean it,' she said, her heart beating like a trapped bird. 'Why should you care about me, Jason? If there's no room in your heart for me, why should you care what happens to me?'

He looked at her for long seconds, then leaned forward and kissed her with infinite tenderness on her lips.

'Because, my dear little idiot,' he said softly, 'the whole problem is that I like you enough not to want to hurt you.' He stood up and loosened his tie, a wry smile curving his splendid mouth. 'Do you realise,' he sighed, 'that I have to spend another whole night next to you again?'

'Is that so awful?' she asked, looking up at him.

'Would you make a man who was dying of thirst sleep next to a beautiful crystal fountain?'

'Oh, Jason—'

'No more!' he warned, laying a stern finger on her lips. 'You could never accept the sort of relationship I want, Storm.'

'How do you know?' she asked desperately. 'Maybe—'

'Maybe nothing.' He unbuttoned the beautiful silk shirt and pulled it off, revealing the velvet-skinned body she knew so well. 'You were born for marriage and a nice house in the suburbs.'

'And you?' she demanded.

Jason looked down at her, the shimmering blue of her dress setting off the honey-gold of her skin.

'That's not for me, Storm. Not yet, anyway. I need my life uncluttered.'

'But you felt differently about Helena,' she accused.

'Yes,' he nodded. 'And I found out the hard way how misplaced my trust had been. We were even discussing marriage, Storm. My God, I dread to think of the misery we would have gone through if we *had* married! Helena was utterly shallow, a woman to whom nothing mattered except her own pleasure and social standing.' He shook his head angrily. 'Do you know what shook me most about the whole affair? That I could have misjudged her so badly. That I could have been such a fool as to place my trust in someone as empty and superficial as

Helena Salisbury. Well, I swore that I would never make the same mistake again, Storm. That I would never place so much trust in another woman. All I want,' he said softly, 'is your desire. And all I can give you is my desire.'

'I could settle for that—if I loved someone.'

'Don't be a fool,' he said roughly. 'How can I make you understand?' He glared at her. 'You mean nothing to me, Storm,' he said in a harsh voice. 'Nothing at all. You're just a woman in my bed—and there've been so many women in my bed that I tend to forget which is which. Do I make myself clear?'

She sat up, blazing with anger and hurt.

'Yes, Jason,' she snapped. 'You make yourself absolutely crystal clear!'

'Good!'

He stalked into the bathroom and slammed the door.

Storm stared after him with furious green eyes. Then she muttered a word not usually heard in polite company, and hurled a pillow with all her force at the bathroom door. It opened, and Jason looked out at her with cold eyes.

'Hell hath no fury like a woman scorned, eh? You just keep your temper, young woman, or I'll put you over my knee.'

Storm went over to the dressing table and brushed her unoffending hair with vicious strokes, tears of anger and misery shining in her eyes. He had thrown her love back in her face. It had cost her so much to admit it to him. And it had cost her even more to reconcile herself to offering him her body. He had even rejected that. She hadn't actually told him how she felt about him—but he knew what she meant. Damn Helena Salisbury!

And by the cold look in those tawny-green eyes, his first priority from now on was going to be ejecting her from his life at the first available opportunity.

CHAPTER EIGHT

THE scene at the start of the race was extraordinary. The big field was now dominated by the balloons of the competitors, over a hundred and twenty great spheres tugging at their mooring ropes, swaying with colourful majesty in the light breeze. The sky was clear and bright, and the fine layer of crisp white snow on the ground had not yet been trampled into slush. Against its pale background, the balloons themselves were brilliant, every shade of the rainbow, most striped in vivid candy colours.

Wrapped in her beautiful coat, Storm watched the amazing scene with wonder. She and Jason had driven out here in the early hours of the morning to inflate the balloon and to prepare for the race. A few minutes earlier, the inspection had taken place. A big group of officials was still making the round, each carrying the all-important clipboard on which points, comments and notes would be made. And a huge crowd had assembled, restrained by the barriers which the police had erected overnight, but excited and happy nonetheless. Even more television crews were in evidence, and the bright morning sky above was buzzing with three or four helicopters and a light aeroplane—all filming the launch of the race.

Storm glanced at Jason. His face was alert, eager, and the hands that checked the nylon rigging were sure and untrembling. Storm, too, was excited—and afraid. This was it—the moment that she had been anticipating and dreading for days. The public address system was still blaring out news, information, advertisements. Competing with it from the other end of the field was a military band, thumping out a succession of popular hits, including (Storm was amused to hear) *Up, Up and Away*. The air was alive with a tingling excitement, sharp with the clean smell of meths from a hundred and twenty burners. There was a sudden bang, and a bright orange flare arced into the blue sky. Jason turned to Storm with eager eyes, and reached out for her hands.

'We're off,' he smiled. Impulsively, she leaned forward to accept his kiss.

'Good luck,' she whispered.

'Good luck,' he answered, his eyes holding hers. 'Do you forgive me for last night?'

'No,' she said with a wry smile. There was a roar from the crowd, and they both turned. The first balloon was away, a beautiful white-and-red bubble lifting swiftly away from the ground. They watched, fascinated. The balloons were being launched individually, according to a complicated system of handicaps. Jason had explained to her that the judges could add minutes or dock them according to variety of factors—appearance, sportsmanship, style—so that the first balloon to touch down in Konstanz was not necessarily the winner. That would only be known after all the variables had been worked out and reduced to a single figure—the 'time' of the race. 'Most bicycle races, like the Tour de France,' he had informed her, 'are run on the same principle.'

Another balloon soared into the air, accompanied by another joyful shout from the crowd. Storm's blood was racing. There was something superbly exhilarating about the sight, something so symbolic of the human urge to free man from the bonds of gravity, to fly! She found that her knees were trembling. Another balloon, a scarlet one, had lifted off now, and the three beautiful craft had formed an uneven line in the clear sky, heading purposefully north-west to the Alps. The enraptured crowd were getting their money's worth. Closing her eyes and muttering an incoherent prayer, Storm fished for her camera and began photographing the event. Two more balloons were up now, the little dark shapes of their baskets hovering beneath them. And then their own timekeeper was preparing to cast off their mooring rope.

'*Pronto?*' he called, holding aloft his stopwatch. Jason nodded, hands ready at the burner, and the official slashed through the rope with a hatchet. At once, Jason opened the burner, and with a roar they were rushing up into the sky. Storm clung to the rigging, her heart beating wildly, as the Campo Graziano receded beneath them. The crowd were waving handkerchiefs and hats, and she stared back at the fantastic scene—a sea of brilliant balloons, eagerly waiting the signal to soar skywards. Within seconds they had risen to a thousand feet, the great crimson and turquoise dome above them hauling them effortlessly into the crisp air. Away to their right, Cremona lay stretched out, the orange of its mediaeval roofs contrasting with the greens and russets of the countryside. She met Jason's laughing eyes, and they hugged each other. Then he passed her the beautiful sealskin gloves he had bought in London, and tugged her fur hat down over her blonde hair, which was blowing in the wind.

'It's going to get pretty cold,' he warned her.

She peered over the edge of the basket. The fertile plain of Lombardy lay below them, fields ready for the autumn harvest, long patches of white snow, the bright squiggle of a river here and there. Already they had reached three thousand feet. Ahead of them, the first balloons were strung out like beads on a giantess's necklace, or magical fairy lanterns. She was astounded to see how far they had already come from Cremona. The big field was just a distant patch of colour now, and a long row of balloons extended behind them, rising up from the outskirts of the city. It was an eerie and wonderful sight. Storm focussed on them through the viewfinder of her camera, took several shots, then turned to Jason. He grinned at her from the burner, his magnificent face joyful, and she pressed the shutter instinctively. A great shot. With a sudden chill she wondered whether that would be all she would have of him, once this race was over.

Within a few hours, the orderly line of balloons had completely dispersed. In the distance, two or three bright specks were visible, but to all intents and purposes, they were alone in the sky. It was a silent, beautiful world. The autumn air was fresh and cool, but they had encountered almost no cloud so far, and a following breeze ensured that they were making good speed towards the Swiss border. By lunchtime they were passing over Milan, a vast, sprawling grey mass beneath them. Now they began to encounter more rivals. Each balloon had to be logged by an observer in the centre of the city, and Jason released air so that they came down to a few thousand feet over the rooftops and streets. It was a city of tinted glass and white concrete, faceless and modern. In the middle of the city, incongruous among all the modernity, the great grey cross of the Cathedral lay spreadeagled. They passed over its spires and over the big square, thronged with sightseers. They ate a hurried meal of cold chicken, washed down with hot coffee from a Thermos, and soon the last straggling suburbs of Milan were fading behind them.

They had exchanged few words since their departure from Cremona. Last night's harshness still ached in Storm's heart, and their quarrel—if you could call it that—had left them both subdued and unsmiling. For the most part, Storm had leaned on the edge of the wickerwork, and had stared downwards, trying to lose herself in the enthralling beauty of the scenery below. The landscape was gradually becoming more rugged. Green fields were giving way to a wild, upland country-side of rocks and woods. They had also begun to notice snow beneath them again. By two in the afternoon they were approaching their first real mountains, drifting low through the valleys, on a level with the peaks. Ahead of them, a wide valley led down into a plain, and a long stretch of steel-blue water.

'Lake Como,' Jason told her. 'This is where the Alps begin.'

'Are we making good time?'

'Pretty good,' he nodded, checking their chrono-meter. 'We should be at the highest point in the Alps by around five o'clock. We'll be over Zurich by dawn—we might touch down for a few minutes if we're running short on fuel. Then across to Konstanz, probably by mid-morning.'

They drifted down the long valley in the bright afternoon sunlight. As they neared the lake, an eagle floated a few dozen feet below them, and Storm gazed down, fascinated, at the huge bird, its wing-feathers moving imperceptibly as it drifted on the high air-currents. Jason came to her side, and they watched together as the big bird soared away to the east, its hooded eyes sparkling in the sunlight. He touched her shoulder, and she turned to take the plastic cup of hot tea he held out to her. His beautiful eyes watched her gravely as she drank.

'Enjoying it?'

'Oh, Jason, it's the most stunning thing I've ever done! It's so—' She gestured at the splendour of the long valley, the peaks drifting by past them, lost for words. 'It's so utterly lovely . . .'

'Storm, I know I was cruel last night. I'm sorry.'

She shrugged, smiling painfully. 'I worked it out in the end,' she said wryly. 'You were being cruel to be kind—weren't you?'

'Something like that,' he admitted. 'Do you understand?'

'I suppose I do,' she said grudgingly. 'But that doesn't mean I forgive you.'

Jason stared at her for a few seconds, then turned to the burner, and sent the violet flame shooting up into the mouth of the balloon with a roar. The edge of the lake was drifting beneath them, and then they were over its glassy blue surface, watching their own crimson and turquoise reflection hovering in the ultramarine depths, soaring over the boats so far down below. At the other end of the long, scimitar-shaped lake, Storm could see the mountains rising upwards to purple peaks in the distance.

'Are those the Alps?' she wanted to know.

'The foothills of them,' he nodded. In the distance, across the western leg of the valley, two balloons were visible, dots of yellow and blue against the grey-greens of the rock.

The long blue sheet of water passed steadily away beneath them, and Jason opened the burner again. They were rising constantly, Storm noticed. She checked the altimeter. Eight thousand feet! Alarmed, she looked over the edge. They seemed to be the same height above the ground. She looked up at Jason, who was watching her face with ironic eyes.

'The ground's rising,' he told her. 'As the mountains get higher, so we have to get higher.'

'Oh,' she said, glancing apprehensively at those jagged purple peaks in the distance. 'There's a lot of cloud up there,' she said, trying not to sound cowardly.

He nodded, his eyes serious.

'Yes. Snow clouds. I hope it's not going to be snowing—or storming—by the time we get there.'

A little chill settled in Storm's stomach.

'Storming? How would we manage in a storm?'

Jason pulled a face. 'We'd have to put down if it got too bad. The weather reports indicated that we should miss all the bad weather.' He glanced up at the long range of sharp-toothed mountains ahead, fished the binoculars out of one of the duffel-bags, and stared intently through them at the clouds. 'Switch on the radio,' he commanded. 'There'll be a weather forecast in five minutes.'

The last stages of a symphony concert were in progress on the radio, and the passionate yet peaceful strains of a Beethoven symphony made a perfect musical score to the high voyage they were making. The weather forecast was in Italian, too rapid and fluent even for Storm to follow. Jason listened intently, his face serious. As it ended, he ignited the burner again, and the big balloon soared higher into the air. Despite the brightness of the sun on their faces, it was now distinctly cool, and Storm glanced longingly at the row of Thermos flasks in the basket. As he cut off the burner, he gave her a grave smile. 'We've just crossed the Swiss border,' he informed her.

'Hooray,' she said drily. 'What did the weather forecast say?'

'There's a big snow-storm brewing,' he said with a sigh.

'Oh,' she commented, and stared at the Alps ahead. The peaks, she could see now, were touching the blanket of dark cloud. 'What are we going to do?' she enquired.

'Well,' he said thoughtfully, 'most of the competitors will put down somewhere this side of the Alps. Bellinzona, or maybe San Bernardino.'

'Most?'

'The real diehards will try and sail under the bad weather—or over it, or through it.'

'And they'll get to the finishing post first?' she concluded.

He shrugged. 'Probably. It depends how long they're delayed by the storm—whether they get blown off course, maybe even forced to ground somewhere in the mountains. It could be quicker to wait until the bad weather's over.'

'And what are we going to do?' she repeated.

His tawny eyes were amused. 'Are you getting cold feet?'

'I'm getting cold everythings,' she admitted, hugging her gloved hands.

He nodded. 'That's the altitude. Tell me if you feel queer, Storm.'

'I'll definitely feel queer if we have to fly through a storm,' she told him sarcastically.

He smiled.

'Well, let's wait till we're a bit closer and make our minds up then,' he suggested, and Storm nodded agreement.

She glanced at his face, the aristocratic, level-eyed face she had come to know so well over the past weeks. Relations between them were strange, strained—as though they were recently introduced strangers. And apart from that one joyful hug, she noticed that Jason had avoided touching her—even coming near her. Which was surprisingly easy in the basket, which was filled with gear, and amazingly roomy. Having once realised that she had become emotionally involved with him, Storm guessed, Jason had decided to leave her absolutely alone. There was little doubt in her mind that as soon as he possibly could, he was going to free himself of her. For good.

'Stop moping,' he interrupted her sad reverie. 'From here on, the scenery is really spectacular!'

Storm awoke with the feeling that something was going horribly awry. Confused and headachy, she could not at first understand where she was—then the sound of the wickerwork creaking and the cold whistle of the wind in the rigging brought it all back to her. The race! And their decision to press on through the snowstorm! She sat up, her sleeping-bag falling away from her, and brushed a layer of fine snow off the nylon. Their little basket was swaying rather uncomfortably in the lurid light.

She shook her head to clear away the muzziness. San Bernardino—they had put down there. A beautiful Alpine village, complete with stocky mountain cattle and goats, their bells clonking musically. That had been at three o'clock. She checked her watch. Five-fifteen. The violet tongue of the burner roared up into the bright cavern of the balloon, and the basket heaved underneath her. San Bernardino—where an eager crowd of spectators had informed them that all the other balloons had decided to press on over the Alps while the daylight held.

'Only a few minutes ahead of you, *signore*,' they had assured Jason, 'the leader is not more than half an hour in front of you.'

Again, they had checked the weather forecast. According to the Swiss announcer, the snowstorm wasn't due until the next morning. And while Jason had stared up at the mountains forty miles ahead, Storm had said to him urgently, 'Let's go on! We'll never win if we sit it out here!' And as he had stared at her, pondering, another balloon had drifted overhead, heading straight for the Alps.

And they had chosen to go on. Storm raised herself, feeling the cold bite into her. After they had left San Bernardino, she had curled up against the wickerwork for a nap. She had slept for almost two hours. The basket swayed rather sickeningly underneath her as she staggered to her feet. Again, Jason ignited the burner and the bright sword stabbed upwards in the heavy yellow light. She came over to him and clung to his broad shoulders. The cloud ceiling was very low over them, a heavy layer of black cumulus that was shedding snow heavily. The great bulk of the balloon over them kept most of the snow out of the basket, but it was bitterly cold. Through the driving snow, Storm could see the magnificent, jagged peaks of a mountain, barely a thousand feet below them. A lurid yellow light was shining from the west, but the sky was dark and forbidding.

'How are we doing?' she asked Jason, holding him tight.

A strong arm slipped around her waist and pulled her to him. 'Not too good,' he admitted.

'God, I'm sorry I slept for so long,' she said. 'I didn't mean to—'

'That's okay,' he smiled, and she caught the glint of his teeth. 'The altitude does that to you. We're about ten thousand feet high right now.' She started as a distant lightning flash illuminated a vast valley to their right for a lurid second. A gust of wind shook the basket again, sending a shower of snow spraying into the basket, and the balloon bounced gravely in the air, like a beach-ball bobbing on an ocean swell.

'I'm trying to get above this cloud,' he told her, hugging her close as she staggered. 'But we can't seem to get through the snow. There's probably a hundred-weight of snow on top of the balloon, for one thing.' He reached for the burner, and the fierce heat of the flame seared upwards for long seconds. The balloon surged, hauling the basket heavily upwards, then rocked horribly to a standstill. In the strange light, Storm could see that they were drifting along between two majestic peaks, into a great valley that extended downwards into the snow-driven darkness beyond. Her teeth had begun to chatter, and she was feeling distinctly breathless—the altitude, she guessed.

Jason muttered a curse, and tried the burner again. This time, the great balloon heaved upwards, buoyed up by the rapidly rising hot air, and they surged up into the cloud layer. At once they were cloaked in thick, icy mist, unable to see more than a few inches in front of their noses. The violet flame illuminated the white, icy-wet universe luridly, and Storm could feel the basket heave upwards against her feet. She pressed her face into the warmth of Jason's chest, beginning to feel genuinely alarmed. The snow was driving wildly around them, filling every crease of their clothing. It was bitterly cold, each breath searing Storm's lungs like cold fire.

And then the cloud had whipped away from them, and they were dropping down into the valley, defeated. Jason tugged at the lever fiercely, and the burst of flame buoyed them up again. Another flicker of distant lightning outlined a savage triangular peak ahead of them, towering over a thousand feet above the balloon into the black cloud on high. She gasped out loud.

'Oberwald,' he said quietly. 'It's nearly twelve thousand feet high.' The landscape just visible through the snow was magnificent and terrible—a sea of peaks and cols, separated by vast empty valleys and huge crevasses.

'Why can't we get through this cloud?' she asked, staring up into his face. 'Is it the snow on the balloon?'

'Yes—and the altitude itself. The burner isn't nearly as efficient at this height.' He looked down at her, brushing the snow off her hair with a gentle hand. 'It's not turning out too well, Storm. I made the wrong decision at San Bernardino.'

'*We* made the wrong decision,' she corrected him. 'I talked you into it—remember?'

'I'm not sure what's going to happen to us,' he said, his eyes calm and fathomless on her. 'If anything happens to you, I'll never forgive myself. You shouldn't even have been here—you should be sitting safely in London, drinking hot tea.'

'I'm here because I want to be here,' she corrected him, a lump rising to her throat. 'I wouldn't have missed this for worlds, Jason.'

He reached down, pressing his cold lips against her face in a tender kiss that made her heart tremble.

'Bless you, Storm,' he smiled. 'Have I ever told you what a magnificent woman you are?'

'Not recently,' she smiled tremulously. The basket swayed horribly in a snow-heavy gust of wind, and she clutched at him.

'You're magnificent, Storm,' he said, his old smile carving fascinating lines at the corners of his mouth. He drew her close to him, and this time the kiss was more thorough. Their lips were icy, but after a moment his were warm and fierce, thrusting against hers with a message that was undeniably, bone-meltingly, sexual. Oblivious to the storm, the snow, the danger, she clung to him, aware only of his body hard against hers, his arms holding her tight and passionately. Like brandy, his kiss spread through her system, warming and melting her, setting a bright flame glowing in her. Then the basket swayed and creaked wildly, and Jason broke away to grasp at the burner with quick hands. As the flame roared, Storm saw the jagged peak rush past them, feet away from the fragile bottom of their basket. Another razor-edge peak drifted, silent and deadly, out of the whirling snow, and sped past them. The jaws of a great valley were open below them, and in the failing light she could see huge peaks rising around them, towering over the little balloon like giants frowning horribly at some minuscule human intruder into their realm.

Under the influence of the burner, the balloon lifted heavily and reluctantly. Again, a cruel white blade of rock rose out of the snow ahead to slash silently past them. It was almost impossible to tell what was ahead of them now.

'Talking of hot tea,' Storm quivered, groping in the now confused bottom of the basket for the Thermos, 'I'm in need of a little sustenance . . .' She found the smooth shape, unscrewed the cap, and passed it to him. 'We won't bother with cups,' she said wryly. Jason drank, grinned his thanks, and passed the flask back to her. The tea was lukewarm and weak, but it put new life into her. She went back to Jason, slid her arms around his taut waist, and clung to him.

'Are we going to win the race?' she enquired.

'The race?' he repeated. 'To hell with the race! I'm more concerned with getting you safely back to civilisation right now.'

'And you,' she said in a small voice.

'You're my only worry, Storm,' he said, holding her head against his cheek. 'For myself, I wouldn't care— but you oughtn't even to be here.' He kissed her roughly. 'I'm going to get you back safe, I swear it.'

'I know you will,' she said, her heart filled with joy at his words. 'But the race,' she said miserably. 'It meant so much to you!'

'No,' he said quietly. 'It didn't—not the race itself.

Not even going up in the balloon. I simply needed to think my way through that horrible trial—and all the bitterness it left in me.'

'And have you?'

'I think so,' he smiled. 'Thanks to you.'

'To me?' She blinked at him. 'Why to me? Have—'

A jagged white mountainside rushed out of the wind-blown snow towards them, and Jason snatched at the burner. This time the roar of the flame hardly lifted the balloon at all, and Storm buried her face against his shoulder as the savage wall of rock hurtled at them, convinced that this was the end, and praying inarticulately, instinctively glad that she was with him at this moment. They cleared the edge of the rock by a few terrifying feet, and soared heavily into the chasm beyond. The burner was roaring constantly now, its spear of flame vivid in the white chaos around them. Against the sound, Jason shouted to her, 'There must be half a ton of snow on top of the balloon by now. She's not rising at all now!'

The blizzard had worsened, and the light was becoming dim now. Storm stared at him through the angry wisps of snow that the wind was driving between them.

'Can't we jettison some of our gear?' she asked.

'It's all lightweight stuff,' he said, his eyes tense and worried. 'It wouldn't make much difference. What we need is to get that snow off.'

'How?'

'I've got no idea,' he said, his face bitter and angry. 'God, I'm sorry about this, Storm.'

'Don't be, Jason. I'd rather be with you here than anywhere in the world right now.

'Don't be crazy,' he said, smiling despite his worry.

'I mean it,' she said, holding his arm, and looking up at him with deep green eyes. 'If I knew you were in danger up here, darling, do you think I could be happy?'

'Storm—' he said, reaching out for her. Suddenly the blizzard intensified, the snow battering at the balloon like deadly, soft boxing-gloves wielded by some malevolent giant, driving them inexorably downwards. Jason ignited the burner desperately, and the flame stabbed up into the whirling snow that was filling the cabin. Then a vicious gust hurled a suffocating spear of snow and ice across them, blinding them and whipping out the violet flame.

'Hell's teeth—the burner's out!' he shouted, and Storm stumbled against him, her face stinging with snow.

'What's going to happen to us?' she gasped blindly. She could feel that they were falling, drifting steadily downwards through the blizzard. He held her tight, sheltering her face against his chest.

'With any luck, we'll land in soft snow,' he told her urgently. 'There might be a village nearby—and we've got our emergency rations.' As they sank through the icy air, Storm felt a sob rising in her throat. At all costs, she must tell him now how much she loved him—now, before it was too late to say anything.

'Darling—' she gasped.

Jason unfastened his leather coat, wrapping it around her, and tried to shelter her in his arms.

'When we hit the ground,' he told her rapidly, 'and if we get separated—you lie still. Understand? Just don't move. I'll come looking for you. Got it?'

'Yes,' she said. 'Jason, I want—'

A giant's vast white hand swung up out of the whirling

ice beneath them, smashed into them with monstrous force, sent them sprawling in agony into the white void below.

Storm came to her senses in deep snow, her teeth chattering like machine-guns. The blizzard was howling across the rough, steeply sloping ground where she lay. *Where was Jason?* She staggered to her feet, calling his name. Her panic sent energy racing through her frozen limbs, and she floundered desperately forward, oblivious to the snow lashing her face or the rocks against which she stumbled. The altitude was making her head spin, and she became aware that the fierce wind was whipping her calls out of her lips and hurling them into the chaos around her. She could dimly see the high shape of a peak just ahead, but everything else was obliterated in the snowstorm. Of the balloon, or Jason, there was no sign. And it was impossible to work out from which way she had come. Remembering his final instructions suddenly, she sank to her knees again. The cold was acute, and she slowly became aware of aches and bruises all over her body. The balloon must have landed somewhere up above, on the peak beside her, throwing her down on to this sloping piece of rock. For all she knew, hideous drops of thousands of feet might lie on either side of her. And Jason? Was he looking for her, even now, shouting her name into the driving snow? Or was he lying unconscious on the ground, perhaps badly injured?

Huddled against the snow, she agonised for long minutes. At last, aware that the cold was going to paralyse her limbs pretty soon, she made up her mind to press on, at least as far as the peak ahead. She blundered forward again, squinting her eyes against the driving needles of snow and ice, desperately praying that Jason would be alive, waiting for her somewhere in the chaos ahead. The last of the light was beginning to fail, and she knew that once darkness came, neither of them would have any chance of surviving the night on this unnamed, bare mountainside. Even if they found each other, it would be chancy—but she knew that if she could once get her arms around Jason's powerful shoulders and bury her face against his chest, her strength would be redoubled.

Clumsy and stiff with the cold, she clambered up the slope. It was horribly treacherous ground, a scree of sharp rocks covered with light snow, and she stumbled and fell painfully several times. Then she fell against something smooth and cold. She brushed the snow away with frantic haste—it was their altimeter, smashed and useless. Alas for their emergency rations—they would be scattered for hundreds of yards across the mountainside, irrecoverably lost. But the altimeter gave her new hope. The balloon—and the man she loved—must be somewhere in the vicinity. She scrambled upwards again, her heart pounding. She came across more debris lying half buried in the gathering darkness. Again and again she called Jason's name into the wild snow, until her voice was hoarse; and then—

He came looming out of the darkness ahead, arms outstretched for her. Sobbing, she rushed to him, flinging herself into his embrace.

'Oh, Jason—thank God you're alive!'

He pressed icy lips to her face, his arms tight around her, and held her without speaking. When her shuddering had begun to ease off, he looked down at her.

'We can't stay here, Storm. We've got to find some sort of shelter—even if it's only a rock overhang. Can you walk?'

'I'm fine,' she smiled through her tears.

He kissed her again, roughly and hard.

'Thank God I found you,' he said. 'I was so afraid you might be—' He stopped, shaking his head, and looking up with squinting eyes into the driving snow. 'Come on,' he said, 'let's get moving.'

CHAPTER NINE

CLINGING to Jason, Storm stumbled onwards through the blizzard, her mind slowly becoming as numbed and dull as her legs. A weary hopelessness had begun to settle inside her—an exhaustion that was draining her strength inexorably. The man beside her was a tower of strength, and she leaned more and more on his indomitable will as they made their stumbling way down the treacherous scree, the hurling snow lashing at them with insensate venom.

Whenever she stumbled, his strong arms were there to catch her, raise her to her feet, and urge her onwards; but she was becoming weak—partly through the delayed shock of their crash, which had now begun to hit her. Her legs seemed to be filled with lead—they dragged in the heavy snow, and she was too weak to lift them over obstacles, and her shins crashed painfully into the sharp rocks. Except that she was becoming dulled to the pain. Dulled to everything.

Even the bitter cold seemed to be fading, leaving a total numbness in its wake.

'Come on, girl,' begged Jason as she stumbled again, her hands clasping feebly at his arm. She rose again, took another pace, and then was stumbling to her knees against the rock. It was almost too dark to see Jason's face as he stooped over her, trying to rub some life back into her legs with his gloved hands.

'We've got to keep going, darling,' he said urgently.

'We can't simply lie here—we'll be dead in hours.'

'I can't,' she panted. 'Oh, Jason—it's so hopeless! Where are we? Where are we going to? We don't even know what we're looking for—'

'Shelter—a little overhang of rock, maybe even a shepherd's hut—anything that'll shelter us from the snow.' He lifted her in tireless arms and pressed his cold face against her cheek. 'Please, darling,' he said in her ear, 'don't let me down.'

She lay in his arms, exhaustion washing over her, the snow falling into her upturned face.

'That's the second time you've called me darling,' she said dreamily, her green eyes hazy.

'I'll call you anything you like,' he said with a wry smile, 'as long as it gets you moving. Please, Storm!'

She tottered up on to legs that were rubbery and almost useless, and tried to drag strength up from some cellar in her being.

'You're wonderful,' said Jason, a note of triumph in his voice. 'Hang on to my waist—I'll put my arm around your shoulders. Now, let's keep moving. This storm is getting a lot worse.'

'I'm glad to hear that,' she stumbled. 'I thought it was just me.'

In the gathering darkness, they could just tell that the steep slope had begun to level out now, and the ground, as far as they could tell under the thick snow, was more even. But it was ferociously cold now, and the only area in Storm's body which still retained any feeling—her face—was aching. Her blonde head began to droop against Jason's shoulder as she walked . . .

In her dream, they were back in the balloon. None of this horror had happened to them—they were up in the warm air, and she was lying against the firm wickerwork, her head swaying to the steady movement of the balloon. Or was it a balloon? No, it wasn't the soaring smoothness of the balloon's motion she was conscious of. It was the steady tread of something living. A horse maybe? Yes. The carriage. She could even hear the silver bells, though she couldn't hear the clop-clop of the horse's hoofs echoing down the empty streets of Cremona. And there was Jason, magnificent in evening dress, his tawny eyes watching her with that half-smile that always sent shivers down her spine . . .

Reality returned slowly, unwillingly to her mind. The storm. The snow. The darkness. And the cold—terrible, penetrating cold that was squeezing the life out of her. She discovered herself in Jason's arms, her head lolling under his chin—she could hear his breath coming fast and ragged as he bore her through the snowstorm with untiring, safe arms. God, she couldn't let him do this! How long had he been carrying her?

'Put me down,' she demanded weakly. 'Put me down!'

'Shush!' His chin was rough against her temple.

'I can walk,' she insisted with feeble petulance. 'Put me down, Jason—'

'You couldn't walk two paces,' he said, his voice rough and tired. 'Don't struggle like that, Storm, for God's sake.'

'Put me down,' she gasped, trying to thrust him away with irrational, nerveless arms. 'I want to be down—you'll kill yourself like this!'

'Shut up,' he said grimly, bowing his head against the whipping snow. For some reason born out of exhaustion and shock, a puny rage had gripped her. She beat at his shoulders, with her fists, cursing.

'Put me down, damn you! I want to be put down—'

'I'll put you over my knee if you don't stop squirming,' he spat out venomously.

Storm tried to pound at his face with numb hands.

'You bastard,' she gasped in weak fury, 'I hate you!'

'I don't feel too kindly towards you,' he snarled, clutching her even tighter, and stumbling onwards through the blackness.

'I've always hated you,' she sobbed, giving up the struggle at last. 'I hated you from the moment I first saw you! You—you—'

Jason almost fell against a rock, and she clutched at his neck desperately, barely interrupting her stream of fury.

'You arrogant, *arrogant* fool,' she gasped. 'I hate everything about you! Do you hear? I hate you!'

'For God's sake shut up,' he told her harshly, his voice heavy with exhaustion.

'I won't shut up,' she blubbered irrationally. 'I want to be put down—I don't want you even to touch me—'

'Right—I'll drop you down the next crevasse we come across, okay?'

'That would suit me just fine,' she snarled. Or thought she snarled. Had she really said that? Funny, she couldn't quite remember whether she had said it, or just thought it. Funny. She decided it would be best to say it anyway, just to make sure. After all, she had *meant* to say it. No sense in not saying it, once she had thought of it. Quite a cutting comment, as a matter of fact. Oh yes, that was quite a gem. That would cut him. That would show him. She chuckled to herself. The arrogant pig— that would show him what she was made of! She opened her mouth—what was it again? She had forgotten her comment. Her priceless comment, the one that was

going to show him what she thought of him. It was gone.
Damn it all . . .

Jason was sitting opposite her in the carriage, his eyes
sparkling with amusement. Now she could hear the
clop-clop of the horse's hoofs. He was being ironic with
her—he was always being ironic. Damn him! And then
she remembered her comment, the priceless one.

'That would suit me just fine,' she said, half opening
her eyes against the driving snow.

'What would suit you just fine?' he gasped. Storm
couldn't remember. She couldn't even remember. The
whole thing was so damned hopeless, anyway . . . A tear
of self-pity rolled down her cheek, and was whipped
away by the wind. 'I hate you,' she sobbed. 'Do you hear
me? I hate you, Jason!'

And then she was sliding to the ground, her strength-
less legs folding up beneath her. Anger surged through
her feebly. He was going to leave her to die, here in
this never-ending snowstorm! How could he be so
callous?

'What have you put me down for?' she demanded.

'A hut,' he gasped, the wonder coming through the
roughness in his voice.

'Pick me up,' she demanded, not understanding him.

'You wait here,' he commanded, his breath coming in
huge, exhausted gasps. 'I'm going to try and find the
door.'

'Don't leave me!'

But her squeal was lost in the wind. She stretched out
her hands to him in misery—and touched a wall. The
cold, rough, unmistakable wall of some human habita-
tion. Then the last words Jason had uttered percolated
through her tired mind. A hut! He had brought them to a

hut! She lay back in the snow, joy seeping slowly and
steadily through her.

They stumbled through the doorway together into the
darkness of the hut, slamming the door behind them
against the howling of the storm. Storm leaned against
the rough walls, too tired even to think, as Jason groped
through the dark, blundering against some heavy piece
of furniture with a curse. A match scraped; the little light
flickered, grew, turned into the comforting soft glow of
an oil lamp. Storm stared around the shadowy room with
tired eyes.

'What is this place?' she asked.

'A goatherd's hut—I think. There ought to be firewood around somewhere.' She stared around the place,
infinitely grateful for its shelter. It was sparsely fur-
nished; a big table, two or three rush chairs, a long, low
bed that appeared to be made of something like brack-
en, a crude stove. For all its roughness, the place had
some homely touches—bright curtains at the windows, a
large religious painting on one wall.

'Where's the goatherd?' she asked, sliding into a
chair, her body still unfeeling and numb.

'Aha!' Jason had unearthed a large bundle of faggots
in one corner, and he dragged it across to the stone-
surrounded fireplace. 'We'll soon be warm. The goatherd? He'll be down in the village, like all sensible
people. Perhaps ten or fifteen miles away.' He piled the
firewood into the grate with sure hands. 'This will be his
pasturing hut—he'll spend a few nights at a time here in
the summer, when he brings his goats up to graze.' He
reached for the matches, and held the little light to the
splintered wood. 'Besides which, these places come in

very handy for emergencies such as the present one.' He grinned tiredly up at her as the yellow flame started to flicker tentatively at the pile of wood. A sudden rush of joy burst through Storm's heart, and she slid forward on to her knees, holding out her arms to him. He held her tightly, oblivious of the snow that covered their hair and clothes. In the silence, the wind howled around the thick log walls of the hut, as though robbed of its prey, and the fire slowly crackled into life. She drew a deep breath as sobs threatened to rack her, and Jason drew back a little, smiling at her with amused eyes.

'What's there to cry about now?' he wanted to know. 'I've got you out of the storm, haven't I?'

'I'm so happy,' she said shakily. 'You're marvellous, Jason—I—'

'That's a change,' he said drily, standing up and tugging his heavy coat off. 'A few minutes ago I was the biggest swine on earth.'

'Oh dear,' she said, appalled as memory began to return. 'I didn't know what I was saying—'

'I know,' he said wryly. 'Still, I think you've damn near given me a black eye.'

'Oh no!' Remorse silenced her as he turned away, and began rifling through the little cupboard in one dark corner. Slowly she was becoming conscious of the misery she was in; her clothes were frozen, and her skin was burning agonisingly as circulation gradually returned to her body. She began to shiver, lightly and intermittently at first, then uncontrollably. Hearing the chatter of her teeth, Jason glanced up at her.

'Feeling bad?'

'Terrible,' she chattered.

'You will do,' he said unfeelingly, returning to his

search. 'However, I've got some treasures here.' He
stood up with an armful of things. 'We're going to have
to do this step by step,' he told her, spilling his prizes on
the table. 'First of all—' He uncorked a long black
bottle, sniffed at it, and nodded approvingly. He knelt
next to her, cradling her head in the crook of his arm,
and touching the neck of the bottle to her lips.

'Drink,' he commanded.

'What is it?' she asked suspiciously, her teeth rattling
against the glass.

He grinned.

'Kerosene. Brandy. Who cares?'

Unimpressed, Storm opened her mouth, and he
poured a generous measure down her throat. Liquid fire
seized her tonsils, erupted into molten lava that scalded
its way down into her stomach. As she coughed in blind
agony, he took a swig himself and gasped approval.

'Kirschwasser,' he said, blinking tears out of his eyes.
'Home-made cherry brandy.' Again, the neck of the
bottle touched her lips, and before she could protest,
more of the molten lava was pouring down her throat.
As she coughed this time, she could faintly taste cher-
ries—as though some homicidal maniac had laced cherry
cola with napalm. Leaving her to cough her way back to
breath, Jason corked the bottle, and rummaged among
the things on the table. 'What's this? Porridge?' He
peered into the bag, and then realisation dawned. 'Ah—
muesli. And milk powder. Excellent. Fancy some hot
muesli with kirsch?'

Storm groaned. But she was beginning to feel distinctly better. The fire was steadily growing, filling the little
cabin with warmth, and the agony in her throat and
stomach was turning into a pleasant glow, like bodily

central heating. Even the howl of the storm outside was beginning to take on a cosy sound. She watched Jason as he stirred melted snow in the battered saucepan he had found, and added the contents of the muesli bag. He was beginning to steam, she noticed enviously, and crept forward to join him in front of the fire. She leaned her head against his shoulder as he stuck the saucepan into the bright flames, and they sat in silence, listening to the wind battering at their roof, each lost in their own thoughts.

The gruel was scalding and sweet, and infinitely comforting. As she scraped her spoon on the bottom of the pan, she looked up to find Jason grinning at her.

'What's so funny?' she demanded.

'You are,' he chuckled. 'Five minutes ago, you were dying by inches. You should see yourself now!'

'You're no oil painting yourself,' she told him, looking at his sodden hair and steaming clothes. She sucked the spoon with relish, suddenly feeling a hundred times better.

'Right,' he said briskly, standing up. 'Get your clothes off.'

'What?' She looked at him in alarm.

'You're soaked,' he said patiently. 'And the room's getting just about warm enough. You can't sit in those wet clothes until help comes—so get them off.'

'But I—' He was no longer listening, hauling his shirt over his head. Storm watched in some trepidation as he unzipped his jeans and kicked them off with distaste.

'Wait,' she said in alarm. 'This isn't decent, Jason!'

He looked at her with inscrutable tawny eyes, and sighed.

'We've just been through the jaws of death together,

Storm. Surely we don't have any secrets from each other any more?'

She stared at him. In the firelight he was magnificent, a living bronze statue, his skin velvety and fine. The midnight blue briefs hugged his body shamelessly, and she looked away in dismay.

'You take your clothes off if you want to,' she said sullenly. 'I'm quite happy the way I am.'

He did not answer, and she stared into the yellow flames with the distinct feeling that he was grinning at her. She could hear him hanging his wet clothes over the chair to dry. Nervously she poked at the fire with a twig, then raked her sodden blonde hair back with her fingers.

Powerful hands seized her arms and hauled her to her feet. She yelped in dismay as Jason spun her round. His eyes were bright with amusement. But they were also quite determined.

'I had to carry you God knows how far in a blizzard,' he said calmly. 'I won't be disobeyed now.'

'*Jason*—' she gasped.

He stood back.

'Look, I'm still wearing my pants—okay?'

Her eyes flashed down the magnificent length of his body, and she coloured as she saw the slim blue briefs that clung to him.

'Now,' he said firmly, and his fingers were tugging at the pearl buttons down the front of her once-beautiful wool coat. Hypnotised, she watched the strong, delicate tracery of muscle across his wide shoulders. His skin was incredibly smooth—but under it, the iron-hard muscles pulsed and shifted with masculine power. He turned her around as though she were a tailor's dummy, and pulled the heavy wet thing off her shoulders.

'Jason—' she began nervously as he turned her back again.

'Shut up,' he said calmly, and hauled her cashmere cardigan unfeelingly over her head.

'Jason,' she snapped, 'leave me alone! I—'

With contemptuous ease, he thrust aside the hands that tried to stop him, and began to unfasten the buttons on her silk blouse.

'This is for your own good,' he told her, his beautiful eyes meeting hers with a glint of mockery in their tawny depths.

'God, I hate you,' she mumbled, her cheeks flushing hotly as he tugged the tails of the blouse unceremoniously out of her skirt. 'Leave me alone—I'll do the rest.'

'Why?' he asked coolly. 'I'm rather enjoying this.' He slipped the wet silk down over her arms, and dropped the blouse over the back of a chair. The warmth of the fire licked at her naked skin, and she tried to turn away from him.

'I'm warm enough now,' she yelped, protecting her lacy bra with her arms.

'Isn't that—that garment wet?' he grinned mockingly.

'It's perfectly dry,' she assured him warily.

Unconvinced, Jason pulled her back to him, and took her in his arms. She gasped as the naked skin of their stomachs touched.

'I'm not trying to humiliate you, Storm,' he said gently.

'Then what—'

His sure, gentle fingers had unclasped her bra, and she folded her arms in anguish over her full breasts. Whereupon he calmly tugged off her sodden, once-elegant corduroy skirt.

'*Jason!*' she gasped in horror. 'I'll do the rest—I swear it!'

'Go ahead, then,' he grinned, turning back to the fire. Cursing him mentally, she hauled off her boots and her tights, feeling an inexpressible relief as the wet garments came off. The dry heat of the fire was washing over her skin, easing out the stinging and the aching that was left over from her ordeal.

'Can I—can I keep my pants on?' she asked nervously.

'Naturally,' he said ironically. Which was big of him, considering that they were nearly transparent anyway. It had not occurred to Storm, dressing for the race a few hours earlier, that she would be stripping nearly naked in an Alpine cabin. The big muscles across his back tensed as he hauled the bed across the cabin floor towards the fire. She stood foolishly, covering her breasts with her arms. He looked up at her with incisive tawny eyes.

'Better come to the fire,' he advised. 'Get some warmth into your system.'

Cautiously, she advanced. The bed was low and un-even-looking, but it was surprisingly soft and comfortable. She sat down gingerly, avoiding his eyes. His chuckle was low and throaty.

'Come up to the fire,' he commanded, and tugged her over by her wrist. 'Are you feeling stiff?'

She nodded.

'I'm not surprised. Your body's covered in bruises.'

'So's yours,' she told him, looking at him quickly from under long lashes.

'Come on,' he said drily, 'get right in front of the heat.' Storm shifted uncomfortably, and sat cross-legged in front of the fire. Its warmth flooded over her, a sleepy, sensuous heat that eased away pain and discomfort. Jason moved up behind her, and she felt his hands slip over her shoulders, rubbing the tired muscles at either side of her neck. She tensed instinctively.

'Take it easy,' he growled. 'I'm not going to eat you.'

Slowly she relaxed. His hands were infinitely strong, infinitely gentle, his thumbs easing the tense muscles, rubbing away the strain. Gradually Storm let her arms drop away from her breasts, allowing the firelight to caress the sensitive skin.

'Your skin is like the finest silk,' he said quietly. 'It's exquisite.'

Her head drooped forward as she rocked to the gentle, powerful massage of his hands. She could feel the tension floating out of her. The fire crackled and whispered in front of her, and the blizzard battered vainly at their stout walls.

'Do you remember the last time we sat in front of a fire?' he asked.

She nodded. 'All too well,' she said softly.

He laughed quietly. 'A lot has changed since then, hasn't it, Virtuous Lady?'

'It's been days since you called me that.' She had closed her eyes. His hands had shifted to rub her shoulder-blades, and the sensation was deliciously soothing. 'But what's changed, Jason? Not you, certainly.'

'You're wrong, Storm.' He rubbed gently across her shoulders, then leaned forward to brush the nape of her neck with his lips. She picked her head up, her lips parting.

'I nearly killed you tonight,' he said quietly. 'And all for what? For nothing.'

'Not for nothing—for your race.'

'This snowstorm means the end of the race,' he sighed. 'Practically every balloon in the competition will have been blown off course or grounded by now. There are going to be injuries, search-parties—it's a disaster. The sponsors will call the whole thing off, and re-stage it as a spring or summer race next year.'

'I suppose you'll enter for that,' she prompted.

His eyes were calm.

'No, Storm, I won't. I don't want to race any more. I'm not going anywhere now. I don't need to.'

'Have you—have you worked out what you're going to do?'

'Yes. I'm going back to the law.'

She turned her head to look at him through half-shut green eyes. 'I'm so glad, Jason,' she said seriously. 'You'll be able to help so many people if you do.'

'I hope so,' he said with a smile. 'It's nice to know someone's got confidence in me.'

'Confidence?' She smiled quietly into the fire. 'I've got more confidence in you, Jason, than in the rock of this mountain we're perched on.'

His hands stopped for long seconds on her back. Then he began massaging her again.

'I was in a bad way when I met you, Storm. Worse than you'll ever know. I don't think I've ever been so low. I'll never be as low as that again, that's for sure. I was sinking in my own bitterness.'

'Oh, Jason—'

'And it took someone very special to pull me out, Storm. Someone with a heart as big as an ocean.'

'Me?' she asked in astonishment.

His laugh was close against her shoulder.

'Don't sound so surprised.' He tugged her backwards, and she flopped back on to the bed, her hands instinctively moving to cover her naked breasts. He smiled at her modesty, staring down at her with eyes that flickered in the firelight.

'Do you think yours are the first woman's breasts I've ever seen?' he asked drily.

'No,' she said in a small voice. 'But you're the first man who's ever seen my breasts.'

The smile faded from his face. Then he took her hands in his own and lifted them away from her chest. Her breasts were full, tipped with pink. Jason leaned forward and brushed each satiny bud with his lips. Storm gasped aloud, then held him away with hands that had begun to shake. He shook his head.

'I'm not going to tease you, Storm. There's so much I want to tell you—I just don't know where to begin . . .'

'Jason Bentley lost for words,' she said wryly. 'It hardly seems possible.' She longed to cover her breasts again, but he had her hands firmly in his own. He smiled at her, the shadows drifting into the clefts beside his mouth. He was incredibly desirable, incredibly beautiful.

'It took you, Storm, to show me the way out of the woods I was in.'

'But—'

'Not necessarily by the things you said, or even the things you did,' he smiled. 'Just by what you were—so innocent, so young—yet so very strong.'

She stared up at him in silence, her heart beginning to thud. His eyes caressed her face.

'You're so beautiful, Storm. When you walked in through the door of that warehouse in Whitethorn

Road, with the sunlight glowing in your hair, I could hardly believe my eyes.'

'Jason, I don't—'

The velvety skin of his ribs brushed her breasts as he stooped over to kiss her. His mouth was agonisingly gentle, a caress like an angel's wing, making her giddy, as though she had peered over an immense height.

'You've never kissed me like that before,' she breathed.

'Haven't I? Strange—I always meant to.'

He kissed her throat tenderly, and she sighed, her arms slipping round his neck, pulling him down to lie against her. The fire spluttered and crackled softly to itself. He lay against her, quiet, and they listened to the wind howling across the mountains.

'I've learned a lot from you, Jason,' she said, her mouth against his hair. 'More than I've ever learned in my life, I think.'

'What have I ever taught you?' he asked, and she could feel his smile against his breast.

'To know myself, for one thing,' she answered. 'To feel, to be happy—to—'

'What?' he asked, sitting up and smiling at her with dazzling eyes.

Storm laid her hands against the crisp curls of his chest, and lowered her eyes.

'To what?'

'I don't—' she began, then looked up at him with sad green eyes. 'I don't think you want to hear, Jason.'

'Don't I?' He leaned forward to take her mouth again, a gentle kiss that clung to her lips with sensuous passion. Then he kissed her again, hard and roughly, his arms claiming her with almost savage force. His kiss tore through her senses like wildfire, pouring flame into the centre of her being, setting her very soul alight. Then he rolled on to his back, pulling her on top of him and staring up at her with hungry, adoring eyes.

'Storm,' he breathed. 'What a beautiful name— Storm.'

She looked down at him, fascinated by his male beauty, feeling the powerful length of his body underneath her.

'You saved my life tonight, Jason,' she said in a trembling voice. 'You carried me in your arms—even when I was half mad, and struggling to be free of you—you never let me go—'

'Never,' he grinned. 'And I never will. After all, it's not every man who's granted to carry his whole life in his arms.'

'Jason,' she said, her heart pounding, 'don't tease me like this, please—'

'If you had died out there, Storm, I would have lain down beside you and died there with you.'

'Jason—'

'I'm not teasing you, Storm. I love you. With all my heart, with every fibre and muscle of my body, with every inch of my mind and heart and soul—'

'Oh, my darling—'

She sank into the flames of his kiss, losing herself in him, no longer Storm Calderwood but a soul in the agonising, frighteningly wonderful experience of being fused with another soul. She was dimly aware that she had a body, a body that was nestling with unbelievable delight against the hard power of the man she loved; but most of all, she was conscious of a delight that flooded her spirit, a joy too deep for the flesh, too high for thoughts, that was filling her whole being with light. He loved her! Jason—the only man in the world she had ever loved, the only man who ever could move her— loved her. She sank against him, too happy for words, as he caressed her golden hair with rough, tender hands.

'Don't do this to me, Storm,' he said, and there was a pleading note in his deep voice. She raised her head to look at him. His eyes were blazing with passion, his face tense.

'Don't do what?' she smiled peacefully.

'Don't make me wait—tell me, for God's sake—you do care for me, don't you? You once said you did—'

'Oh, darling,' she said shakily, as his meaning dawned on her, 'I swear you'll never have to ask me that again. I love you, Jason. I've loved you for weeks. I've tried to fight it, as hard as I've ever fought anything in my life—but it was no use. I'm yours, my darling, body and soul!'

His lips claimed hers again, joyful and fierce, and she was suddenly fully aware of their nakedness, their skins touching in the firelight. A deep, sensual shudder passed through her, and she stretched with delicious passion across his hard body.

'You were mine from the first,' he said with a smile that shook her. 'I wanted you so badly, Storm. First as a lover. You're so lovely, so incredibly desirable! I couldn't keep my eyes off you.'

'You can look your fill now,' she said shyly, gazing at him with half-closed green eyes. He kissed her again, caressing her lips with passionate amusement.

'But that wasn't enough. Very soon I knew it wouldn't be enough merely to be your lover. I wanted more than that. I wanted *you*—body and mind. I wanted you at my side, always—to have our children, to make our lives together.'

'What about—her?' she murmured into his throat. 'Helena Salisbury. Do you still think of her?'

'Helena?' He burst out laughing. 'You're not still worrying about her, are you? My poor baby, didn't you hear what I said that night in Cremona? I never loved Helena, never! And how could I possibly be thinking of anyone else now that I'm in love with the most beautiful, most adorable, sexiest—'

Her lips silenced him, first tentatively, then with a growing ardour that made them both tremble.

'Jason,' she whispered in wonder. 'You're so very beautiful, darling. Don't ever leave me . . .'

'Leave you? Yes, when I've left my heart and my brain, when I've left myself and the stars and universe, and gone to some other dimension and age to mourn for ever—*then* I might leave you. But not before!'

'My only darling, I'll be everything you want. I'll make you so very happy!'

'You couldn't fail,' he said, his eyes deep and adoring. 'Will you marry me, Storm?'

'Marry you?' She took a deep, shuddering breath. 'I'll be anything, do anything, as long as I can stay by your side for the rest of my life. I'm yours, my soul—whether you marry me or not.'

'In that case,' he grinned, 'let's just live together.' Then he burst out laughing at the expression on her face. 'My dearest heart, you're going to be the most beautiful bride that ever walked up a cathedral aisle.'

Storm laughed a little through her tears.

'Do you think the mountains are full of couples like us

tonight, darling—making their lives together, building their futures together?'

'Whoever is out in this pitiless night,' Jason smiled gravely, 'there are very few as happy—or as lucky—as us. I hope they take weeks to find us.'

'I don't,' she said with a smile. 'I want to be married to you as soon as possible.' The light in her green eyes left him in no doubt as to her meaning, and he laughed softly and delightedly.

'You're becoming quite wanton, my sweet wife!'

'I probably will do,' she said calmly, but the scarlet in her cheeks belied the coolness of her tone. Jason gathered her in his arms, still laughing, and covered her sweet, oval face with kisses.

'My darling Storm,' he said softly, cradling her against his chest. 'I want to hear all about you. Right now— every detail, from your earliest memories up to the present instant.'

'That won't take long,' she smiled tremulously up at him.

'If you run dry,' he grinned, 'I'll start on my own life story. We've got the rest of our lives, anyway!'

And they were still talking, their voices soft and low and loving, when the dawn rose clear and pink over the mountains, and the first shouts of the rescue party began to echo across the snow-filled valleys.

THE HISTORY OF BALLOONING

Ballooning is more than a sport — it's an addiction. Balloon devotees, such as Jason, have been around for 200 years, always searching for the perfect ascent.

Paris, in 1783, was ballooning's birthplace. Joseph Montgolfier, a papermaker, envisioned a paper-and-linen bag drifting above the trees, but try as he might, his invention would not fly. One night, after seeing his wife throw a paper bag into the fireplace and watching it float up the flue, he was stirred into action. Soon the first balloon drifted over Paris, sustained in its height by the hot air produced by burning wool and straw beneath it. Two months later, as 400,000 people stared in awe, a manned flight took place.

Balloon fever spread rapidly throughout Europe. Jean-Pierre Blanchard delivered the first airmail letter when he flew from England to France — though to stay aloft in the foul weather he was forced to throw everything overboard, including his trousers! Balloons were even used in war. Thaddeus Lowe, a Yankee, became the first "spy in the sky" during the Civil War. His balloon corps flew over enemy lines, with observers dangling in gondolas and telegraphing messages to land-bound troops.

In 1873, while Jules Verne was writing his fictional ballooning adventure, *Around the World in Eighty Days*, balloonists were trying to meet the less ambitious but equally harrowing challenge of crossing the Atlantic Ocean. All who tried failed, either because of raging storms or deadening calm. But eventually, with the advances of propane-fed nylon balloons, oxygen masks and enclosed gondolas, a trio of Americans made a triumphant flight over the ocean in 1978.